From the moment they were born,

Noah's two children had given his life new meaning. Once they were born, it took little more than a toothless smile to brighten his world. And now they were loving little beings who deserved to be loved right back.

By a woman's gentle hands.

He'd try to persuade Dara Mackenzie to marry him.

Dara was the woman God intended him to spend the rest of his days with; his prayers had convinced him, and Noah knew it like he knew the earth would continue spinning.

So somehow he had to convince *her* of that.

For his children's sake.

And…for his own?

Books by Loree Lough

Love Inspired

Suddenly Daddy #28
Suddenly Mommy #34
Suddenly Married #52

* Suddenly!

LOREE LOUGH

A full-time writer for more than twelve years, Loree Lough has produced more than two thousand published articles, dozens of short stories—appearing in magazines here and abroad—and novels for children ages eight to twelve. The author of twenty inspirational romances (including the award-winning *Pocketful of Love* and *Emma's Orphans,* and bestsellers like *Reluctant Valentine* and *Miracle on Kismet Hill*—all from Barbour Books), she also writes as Cara McCormack and Aleesha Carter. A comedic conference speaker, Loree loves sharing in classroom settings what she's learned the hard way. And since her daughters, Elice and Valerie, have moved into homes of their own, Loree and husband Larry have been trying to figure out why some folks think the "empty-nest syndrome" is a "bad" thing....

Suddenly Married
Loree Lough

Love Inspired®

Published by Steeple Hill Books™

STEEPLE HILL BOOKS

ISBN 0-373-87052-3

SUDDENLY MARRIED

Copyright © 1999 by Loree Lough

This edition published by arrangement with Steeple Hill Books.

Printed in U.S.A.

Rest in the Lord, and wait patiently for Him.
—*Psalms* 37:7

To Elice and Valerie, my beloved daughters…
and lifelong friends.

Prologue

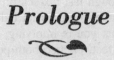

"This is ridiculous," she seethed, slamming the report onto the desk. "I refuse to believe my father could have done such a thing."

Dara stood so abruptly her chair toppled over behind her. Noah Lucas gave the fallen chair a cursory glance before turning his dark-blue gaze to her. "I'm afraid it's all right here in black and white."

Dara uprighted the chair and ran a trembling hand through her hair. "Then...there must be some mistake, because—"

"I've been over these files three times. Numbers don't lie."

Spoken like a true accountant, she reflected.

Ironically, Dara had been drumming that very lesson into her geometry and algebra students' heads since she began teaching at Centennial High eight years earlier. Frowning, she looked from the computer readout to the corporation's checkbook to the year's worth of her father's bank statements. Money—great sums of it—had been moved from the company coffers into Jake Mackenzie's personal account. Hands clasped beneath her chin, Dara paced beside the desk. "Who could have done such a thing?" she wondered aloud. "And why?"

He heaved an exasperated sigh. "I have no idea why the man would do anything so foolish. I mean, surely he realized that sooner or later, he'd be found out." Shaking his head, he added, "How he managed to get away with it through last tax season is a myster—"

Her pacing came to an abrupt halt beside the desk. "I don't like what you're implying, Mr. Lucas."

He got to his feet, planted both powerful palms flat on her father's desk. "I'm not implying anything, *Miss Mackenzie.* My accounting firm was hired by the board of directors to examine…" He smiled patronizingly. "For the sake of protocol, let's just say we were called in to investigate certain, ah, *incongruities* in Pinnacle Construction's books. Lucas and Associates has earned its reputation for being able to solve problems like this."

"Problems like *what?*" Agitated, Dara pointed at the paperwork on the desk. "You call that evidence?" She rolled her eyes. "Innuendo and supposition—that's all you've got there. And I—"

His long-lashed blue eyes narrowed to slits. "Innuendo and supposition?" The intended humor in Lucas's resonant laugh never made it to his eyes. "More than two hundred thousand dollars disappeared in the past eighteen months." He thumped the printout, then nodded at the bank statements. Sarcasm rang loud in his voice when he added, "And by some strange coincidence, that's exactly how much was deposited in your father's savings account."

Dara opened her mouth to protest, to defend her father's good name. But Lucas held up a hand to forestall any attempt at rationalization she might make. "I realize it's not much consolation," he said, "considering the ramifications, but I'm as surprised as you are. Jake Mackenzie's reputation as an honest businessman earned him the respect of his contemporaries up and down the East Coast. Frankly, he's the *last* person I would have suspected of stealing from his own partner."

Gasping, Dara's eyes widened. "How *dare* you call my father a…a…" She swallowed, unable to say the word.

"Thief?" Lucas finished. The blond eyebrow rose high on his forehead. "If you have a better explanation for how the funds got from here—" he nodded toward the big blue checkbook "—to there—" he indicated the savings statements "—I'm certainly willing to hear you out."

No matter how bad things looked—and they looked gloomy indeed—Dara wouldn't let herself believe her father had had anything to do with the missing money. Perhaps Jake's secretary had deposited the money into his account by mistake. Or maybe that new comptroller hired a year or so ago wasn't doing his job properly. It might have been the bank's error.

The excuses amounted to a weak defense. Dara knew it. At best, those possibilities she'd listed might explain one or two erroneous withdrawals and deposits, but *dozens…?*

The ugly truth is, there isn't a good explanation for this mess. But there is an explanation! But she saw no sense in arguing the point, at least not here, not now. The truth will come out in the end, she assured herself, and my father will be cleared of these ludicrous accusations! "So what happens next?" Dara asked, meeting Lucas's icy stare with one of her own.

She hadn't expected the look of sincere concern to furrow his handsome brow. Hadn't expected the broad shoulders to slump as he dropped onto the leather seat of the ancient chair that had once belonged to her grandfather, founder of Pinnacle Construction.

Shaking his head, the accountant steepled both hands beneath his chin. "I expect that's up to Kurt Turner."

Kurt Turner! Dara fumed. But that old fool has been trying to get rid of Dad for years. I wouldn't be surprised if he was the one who deposited all that money into Dad's account!

It dawned on her just then that all this funds juggling had begun about the time Kurt Turner started talking with Acmic Chemicals. The world-renowned agricultural firm had solicited a bid from Pinnacle Construction, and Turner was to have flown to England to discuss the project...a thirty-million-dollar, twenty-five-acre industrial complex. At the last minute, family problems kept Turner from attending the meeting. The company's shaky financial future—and the security of its 106 employees—rested on the outcome of this bid. So, despite the fact that he'd only recently been released from the hospital, Jake Mackenzie insisted on going to England in Turner's stead.

"I'm beginning to smell a rat."

Lucas sat forward, folded those big hands on the desktop. "*Now* we're getting somewhere."

"Excuse me?"

"I called you in here to solicit your help, Ms. Mackenzie. I was hoping we could put our heads together, figure out why your father took the money and—"

"He *didn't* take it, I tell you!"

Lucas drove a hand through his hair, leaving finger-thick streaks in the blond waves. "Tell me something that gives me *reason* to believe that."

Dara sighed and, pointing at the reams of paper on his desk, said, "What can I tell you that you don't think you know?"

He tugged on one corner of his mustached mouth. "As I was starting to say earlier, I want to help you."

She frowned. *"Why?"*

The blue eyes darkened like angry thunderclouds. "You'll find I'm very thorough, Miss Mackenzie." He scrubbed a hand over his face, then said in a gentler tone, "Something troubles me about this investigation."

From the moment they'd said their cool and courteous hellos, Dara sensed Noah Lucas was like a bounty hunter, determined to bring in his man. The look of genuine concern, the slight tremor in his deep voice, forced her to reconsider her first impression of him.

"Well," she began, "I've suspected for some time that Kurt Turner was out to get control of the company."

"But I thought—"

"That because my father made him a partner, they were best friends." She nodded grimly. "That's what everyone thought. The truth was, Dad brought Mr. Turner into the business when it looked as though he might lose everything—his contracting firm, his house, his wife." Her forefingers drew quotation marks in the air. "'If we put our talents together,' Dad said, 'we can double our income.'" She sighed. "He often remarked that Kurt Turner had blueprint ink for blood, whereas Dad was a natural-born salesman."

"Apparently, he was right."

"For a while. But Dad had one major flaw. He paid little if any attention to things like bank statements and tax returns—which is how Pinnacle got into money trouble in the first place."

"How long were they in, ah, 'trouble'?"

"Dad never wanted me involved in the business. But from the little he said, I gathered they'd been having money problems for the past five years or so."

"So the deal with Acmic Chemicals would have saved their bacon."

"I'll say! A thirty-million-dollar industrial complex on twenty-five acres would have put them right back on the map."

"But..."

"But Mr. Turner had family problems, or so he said, and couldn't go to England to seal the deal. Dad insisted on going, even though he'd just gotten out of the hospital."

"Hospital? What was wrong with him?"

"Heart attack." Dara hadn't discussed it, not even once, since that day when her father had sat where Noah Lucas was sitting now. "I did my level best to talk him out of that trip, but he said he had to go, said he owed it to his employees to try to save Pinnacle."

Lucas nodded.

"I think Kurt Turner knew how things would turn out if he let Dad go abroad to cut that deal. What better way to get rid of the competition than to publicly discredit him?"

He shook his head. "I'm afraid I'm not following you."

"The trip to England was one of those 'good news, bad news' stories. The Acmic Chemicals people loved him, and even though they hadn't made the low bid, Pinnacle won the contract…and the stress of cutting the deal cost Dad his life.''

He heaved a deep sigh. "I'm sorry. I didn't know."

Dara would have preferred that in place of the sympathetic, caring tone, he'd continued behaving like the coldhearted shark she'd thought him to be in the first place. At least then she wouldn't be fighting tears right now.

She hadn't let self-pity dictate her actions to this point, and she refused to allow it to control her emotions now. Dara looked around the office, forced herself to see the place she'd so often visited over the years. Dozens of times since the funeral, she'd tried to talk herself into coming here, packing up her father's personal belongings and bringing them home. But there had always seemed to be a valid reason to put it off: weeds in the flower beds; students' papers to grade; a trip to the vet with her cat, Lucy…

Everything looked exactly as he'd left it—a fact that surprised her, since she'd expected Kurt Turner would have assigned the office to someone else by now—except for the plaque on the wall behind his desk: In Memory of Jake Mackenzie, it read, Friend and Father to Us All. Despite her bravado, tears of pride stung her eyes as she acknowledged that he'd *earned* the affection and respect of those men and women who'd commissioned the trophy.

Kurt Turner may well be full owner of Pinnacle Construction now, but Mackenzie blood and sweat had built it. If she had to beg, borrow and spend every red cent she'd saved over the years, she'd replace that missing money.

And if it takes the rest of my days, I intend to clear his good name!

"I wish I could share your confidence, Miss Mackenzie, but it looks as though we have a clear case of embezzlement."

Dara hadn't realized she'd spoken her vow aloud, a fact that only served to increase her distress. She wanted to tell Lucas to get out, right this instant, before he defiled her father's memory any further. Don't shoot the messenger, she reminded herself, citing the age-old proverb; Kurt Turner was the enemy, not Noah Lucas.

He stood, an action that Dara supposed was his way of saying their meeting had ended.

"Thank you for agreeing to see me, Miss Mackenzie. I only wish we'd arrived at a more satisfactory outcome." He extended his hand. "The only thing left for me to do is find out what he did with all that money."

Did he really expect her to shake his hand, after he'd said something like *that?* Fury had Dara gripping the arms of the chair with such force that her knuckles ached. Rising slowly, she faced Lucas head-on. "I realize you have a job to do, Mr. Lucas," she said, retrieving her coat and purse from the chair beside hers, "but so do I." She stopped just short of the door and said over her shoulder, "Since we'll be at loggerheads, you'll forgive me if I don't wish you luck."

Chapter One

The moment she got home from her meeting with Noah Lucas, Dara phoned the pastor's office. "If no one has volunteered to take over Naomi King's Sunday-school class," she said, "I'll be happy to do it."

"Wonderful!" the preacher thundered into her ear. "Stop by the church this evening, and I'll see that you get the materials you'll need."

A little of Scarlett O'Hara's mind-set, she thought, driving to the church, would go a long way in keeping her mind off her problems. She'd worry about the accusations against her father tomorrow. Meanwhile, in the battered cardboard box the pastor had handed her, Dara found keys that would unlock the church basement, the office and the classrooms. The student roster and Naomi's lesson plans were inside, as well, along with a teacher's manual that complemented the workbooks each student had been issued.

She'd taught Sunday school before, but not since her father's death. Dara's last class had been a spirited group of junior-high kids whose pointed questions and heartfelt opinions had left her exhausted yet exhilarated at the end of every class.

Teaching this class of first and second graders would be especially challenging, for Dara would, in effect, be setting down a foundation upon which they would hopefully build a lifetime of spiritual beliefs. In her mind, it was the answer to two prayers: the work involved with preparing for class would keep her from thinking about Noah Lucas's investigation and the teaching itself would fulfill her personal belief that every parishioner should do his or her share to help the church.

She arrived half an hour earlier than necessary and organized the materials she'd use for today's lesson. Then, sitting at the small wooden desk near the windows, Dara prayed: *Father, be with me as I help these youngsters learn about Your will and Your way. Open my mind and my heart to Your word and keep me alert so I'll not miss even one opportunity to glorify You in their eyes. Amen.*

Her intent had been to review her lesson plan until the children arrived. To the casual observer, it would appear she was doing exactly that. But church and Sunday school were the furthest things from her mind as she paged through the teacher's manual on her desk. Rather, Noah Lucas occupied her thoughts. Know Thine Enemy hadn't become a cliché because it was *bad* advice, she'd told herself. And during the past week, she'd made it her business to learn as much as possible about the man who had seemed determined to prove her father had been a thief. Dara had asked anyone who might have come into contact with Noah why he'd come to Baltimore, if he was married, whether he had children—surely a good-looking man like that was married.

Dara lurched with surprise when the fresh-faced six- and seven-year-olds, dressed in their Sunday finest, filed into the room, giggling and chattering as they found places to sit. The moment she saw the wide-eyed innocent faces she knew volunteering to teach this class had been the right thing to do.

There was Pete Chapman and little Tina Nelson; Donny Murphy and Marie Latrell. She'd gone to school with Sammy O'Dell's father, played softball with Lisa Johnston's mother. She knew every child in the room...

Except for two.

Angie and Bobby Lucas.

Alice, the pastor's secretary, escorted the children in and in a discreet tone filled Dara in on their background. The Lucas children had come to town a year or so ago when their widowed father decided to make Columbia, Maryland, the headquarters for his CPA and financial services firm. When he'd registered as a parishioner, Noah Lucas had told Alice he hoped being based in the Baltimore-Washington corridor would triple his clientele within two years. Dara knew enough about the area to believe he could accomplish his goal if he attacked everything the way he'd sunk his teeth into that nasty matter at Pinnacle.

She watched his children carefully. The boy, blond, blue eyed, was the spitting image of his father. Would he be tall and muscular someday? With a thick burnished mustache and a barrel chest?

Dara turned her attention to Noah Lucas's daughter. His wife must have been a dark-haired, dark-eyed, delicate beauty, if her little girl was any indicator.

What must it be like, Dara wondered, growing up without a mother? She'd been twenty-seven when her own mother had died two years ago, and still Dara missed the maternal love that had flowed steadily and easily from parent to child. But to be so small, so young and vulnerable, when death stole a beloved parent... Dara's heart ached for these two motherless children.

They sat side by side, front and center, and folded their hands on the desktops. They were by far the best-dressed, most well-behaved children in the classroom. But there was something about them that gave Dara an uneasy feeling. Was it their tight-lipped, somber-eyed expressions? Or the way they stared straight ahead, as silent as little statues? Looks as though a serious nature runs in the family, she thought, frowning as she recalled their father's grim, taut posture.

"Okay, kids," she called, clapping to get the class's attention. "Let's settle down and get to work."

"Where's Mrs. King?" Marie wanted to know.

Dara smiled as a moment of warm wishfulness fluttered inside her. If only someone could be making this announcement about me.... "Mrs. King's baby was born last Sunday afternoon."

"After Sunday school?"

"That's right. She went straight to the hospital from here."

"Is she all right?" Lisa asked.

"She's fine, just fine," Dara assured her.

"Boy or girl?" Pete demanded, grinning mischievously. "A boy, I hope—we already got too many girls in this town!"

The boys snickered and the girls groaned in response

to his commentary, while Dara smiled fondly. "I hate to disappoint you, Pete, but the baby is a girl."

Tina raised her hand. "Have they named her yet?"

"As a matter of fact, they're going to call her Sarah. Sarah Naomi King."

"Yuck," Pete grumped. "What'd they go an' give her such a sissy name for?"

"Hush," Tina scolded, frowning. "Sarah *isn't* a sissy name. It's beautiful." One hand on her hip, she bobbed her head back and forth. "It's from the Bible," she singsonged, "isn't it, Miss Mackenzie?"

"That's right.... Now, can anyone tell me anything about the biblical Sarah?"

"She was Isaac's mother," Bobby Lucas volunteered.

"But before she was Sarah," his elder sister injected, "her name was Sarai."

"What did she go and change her name for," Pete teased, "if it was so *beautiful?*"

"Because," Angie said, lifting her chin, "God told her husband to change it."

She seemed so pleased and proud to possess knowledge the other children did not have. Was the behavior something her father had encouraged? Or had his straitlaced personality sent Angie the message that this demeanor was required if she hoped to gain his approval?

"Everyone said Abraham was too old and feeble to have more children," the girl continued, "but he believed he could, and because of his faith, God gave him a child," Dara reported in a somber, quiet voice.

These were not ordinary children, Dara decided. Did Bobby play with trucks? Did Angie and her dollies have tea parties? Did they splash in their tub, dunk cookies in their milk and make snow angels? Something told her they did not. Dara could almost picture them sitting inside, noses burrowed in the pages of some edifying book, peeking up only now and again to watch the fun going on *outside*.

Of course youngsters should pray and read the Word, she acknowledged. They should respect their elders and do their chores and work hard in school. But they should never be made to forget that Jesus loved the little children, *because* of the innocent playfulness born into them! What kind of parent was Noah Lucas that he had seemingly discouraged his son and daughter from doing what should come naturally to all kids—enjoying life!

"When is Mrs. King coming back?" Tina interrupted.

Dara sent a quick prayer of thanks heavenward for the question that diverted her from her thoughts. "Well, she's so excited about being a new mommy I don't think even Mrs. King knows the answer to that question."

"Are *you* going to be our teacher?"

She inspected the wide-eyed, expectant faces of her students. "Yes. Yes, I am."

Silence blanketed the classroom. "Good," Pete muttered to the boy behind him, "'cause she's really pretty."

Dara clasped her hands. "Now then, I had intended to talk about the Golden Rule today. Who knows what the Golden Rule is?"

"Jesus said, 'Do unto others as you'd have them do unto you,'" Angie offered.

"Very good," Dara said. "Can anyone tell me what that means?"

"Don't do stuff to other people that you wouldn't want 'em doin' to you?" Pete chanced.

"Absolutely! Someone give me an example."

The children thought about that for a moment. Then Donny shouted out, "Oooh-oooh! I know, I know! Like...if I don't want my sister hogging the swing, I shouldn't hog it, either."

"And if I wouldn't like my brother changing the channel in the middle of a show I'm watching," Lisa added, "I shouldn't do it to him."

Dara walked to the supply cabinet and swung open the doors. "That's right!" She stood in front of shelves that housed colorful stacks of construction paper, blunt-edged scissors, bottles of glue and boxes of crayons. "But it can also mean doing good things."

"Like what?" Marie asked.

"Like helping people finish chores so they can get outside and play sooner, or sharing the last slice of chocolate cake." Wiggling her eyebrows, she winked and gestured toward the cupboard. "Or making greeting cards that will let Mrs. King know how happy we are that she and Mr. King finally got that baby they've been praying for."

Giggling and squealing with glee, the first and second graders grabbed materials from the cupboard and began working on their cards.

"How do you spell *congratulations?*" Tina wanted to know.

Dara was about to print the word on the chalkboard when Bobby Lucas said, "*C-o-n-g-r-a-t-u-l-a-t-i-o-n-s.*"

"Not so fast," Pete complained.

How many first graders could even read the word? Dara wondered as Bobby spelled it again. It was beginning to look like Noah Lucas had the discipline part of fathering down pat. But what about the loving part? she asked herself.

"Thanks, Bob-oh," Pete said, grinning. "How'd you get so smart?"

Dara thought she saw the hint of a smile tug at the corners of Bobby's mouth when he shrugged.

"His name isn't Bob-oh," Angie corrected. "It's Bobby, which is short for Robert."

"You mean *robber*," Pete stuck in. "Your brother stole my pencil."

"Didn't steal it," Bobby defended. "I only borrowed it." He handed it back to Pete, then crossed both arms over his chest.

"'Thou shalt not steal,'" Pete teased, wagging a chubby finger at his classmate.

The statement made Dara think of her father. Heart pounding, she looked around the class, saw that Angie was looking directly at her. For an instant, Dara wondered if the little girl had read her thoughts, for her understanding expression seemed far too old and wise for one so young. But she said, "My mother called him Bobby, right up to the day she died."

Dara wanted to wrap her in a hug—something she suspected her father didn't do nearly often enough—but Angie had already turned her attention back to the artwork. She glanced at Angie's younger brother, who shrugged again and in an equally matter-of-fact voice announced, "Don't pay any attention to her. She says things like that all the time." He raised one blond brow, looking amazingly like his father when he did. "Father says she does it to shock people."

Father says? Dara forced a laugh and ruffled

Bobby's honey-blond hair. "Well," she whispered, "it works. I'm shocked!"

One corner of his mouth lifted in a wry grin. "Pete's right."

"About what?"

The smile that lit his face was contagious, and for a moment, she almost forgot there were a dozen other children around her.

"You're very pretty."

Angie, who had been hunched over Mrs. King's card, sat up straight and gave Dara a once-over. "Yes, yes," she agreed. "You are rather pretty." Furrowing her brow, she added, "Are you married?"

The enrollment forms clearly stated that Bobby Lucas was six years old and Angie was seven. Because they'd been born in the same calendar year—Angie in January, Bobby in December—the children had been in the same grade since preschool. But surely there had been a clerical error, Dara thought, a typo on their registration forms, because neither child behaved even remotely like first graders.

"Father says ladies can sometimes be sensitive to that question. Since you didn't answer, it must mean you aren't married." Angie tilted her head slightly, as if considering all the possibilities. "Have you ever been married? I mean, you're not *divorced* or anything, are you, because Father says divorce is a sin."

Why would his children even be asking such a thing, let alone asking it frequently enough to require adult discussion on the subject? Dara could answer Angie's questions—questions that would not have seemed overly personal or inappropriate if they hadn't been asked in that eerily controlled voice—or she could divert the child's attention. Her father may choose to speak to her like a miniature adult, Dara thought, frowning slightly, but here in my classroom, she'll be treated like a seven-year-old!

"The card you're making for Mrs. King is lovely," she said in an upbeat, friendly voice. "I especially like the pretty house you've drawn there."

"It's like the one we lived in up in Pennsylvania, when my mother was alive." She tucked in one corner of her mouth. "It was a very nice house."

Angie took a deep breath, then said, "It happened when I was four." She put the red crayon she'd been using back into the box, and withdrew a blue one. "It was cancer, you know, the kind that eats your blood."

"Leukemia," Bobby said. But unlike his sister's nonchalant tone, the boy's voice trembled slightly.

"Yes. Leukemia," Angie agreed. "Father says we should try not to think about it, but when we do, we should never be sad because Mother is with Jesus in heaven, where she'll never hurt ever again."

It had been nearly a decade since Dara had taken the psychology courses that helped round out her education major, but Dara recognized repression when she saw— and heard—it. And though she'd been a full-grown adult when her own mother died two years earlier and lost her father just months ago, she understood the importance of mourning openly and honestly. Dara didn't know how or why a loving father would talk his children out of grieving for their mother.

And she understood it on a completely different level: hadn't she repressed her fears that her father might have stolen Pinnacle's money?

She wouldn't even suspect it, if it hadn't been for Noah Lucas! It wasn't hard to believe he could do such a coldhearted thing. Dara's eyes and lips narrowed with anger toward the man who, without ever having met her father, had chosen to believe the row of numbers that said Jake was a thief rather than the daughter who believed in his innocence. That same harsh and judgmental behavior had his own flesh and blood moving through life like windup toys.

Dara had prayed before class began that the Lord would show her what to do, tell her what to say, to help her teach these children His word. These two, especially, needed to hear about His loving mercy now.

Dara slid an arm around the girl's shoulders. "Oh, sweetie," she said, leaning her forehead against Angie's, "of course your mommy is in heaven with God and all His angels." She pressed a soft kiss to the child's temple. "But it's okay to miss her sometimes...."

Angie looked up from her picture and stared deep into Dara's eyes. For a second there, Angie was every bit a seven-year-old girl as her lower lip trembled slightly and a flicker of sadness gleamed in her big dark eyes. Dara felt the fragile shoulders relax, as though a heavy burden had been lifted from them.

But then Angie blinked.

And just that fast, the frosty restraint was back, and she became a pint-size version of a full-grown adult again. It was more than a little frightening to have witnessed the transformation, and Dara shivered involuntarily, because she doubted if she could name one adult who was so self-contained.

Well, that wasn't true. She could name *one*....

"Can I get a drink of water?" Tina asked.

"Sure," Dara said, smiling gently.

"Would you like to see the card I made for Mrs.

King?'' Pete wanted to know. "I drew baby Sarah on it.''

"I'll be right there.'' Reluctantly, Dara drew away from Angie. If the child noticed, she gave no clue. *God bless her,* Dara prayed.

Something told her that in the months ahead, she'd be petitioning the Lord often on behalf of the Lucas children.

"Sorry, Dara,'' the principal said. "I've pulled every string I could get my fat little fingers on. There's just no money left in the budget for you.''

Budget cuts, or had someone on the board heard that her father had been accused of embezzlement and decided it wasn't good press to have a teacher like that working for the Howard County school system?

She took a deep breath. Stop assuming the worst, Dara, she scolded herself. It's your own fault, after all, for asking to be assigned a job in your own district. If she'd taken the teaching job at Wilde Lake instead of Centennial High, she wouldn't be low man on the totem pole now.

"It isn't your fault, John,'' she said, smiling half-heartedly.

"Who'd-a thunk seniority could be an ugly thing?''

"Better watch it,'' she warned, wagging a finger under his nose. "If the kids hear you breaking the rules of grammar that way, they'll—''

"They'll what?'' he teased. "Most of 'em have been abusing the King's English since right after they learned to say 'Dada'!''

Dara and her boss laughed for a moment, until the seriousness of the situation shrouded his cramped, crowded office.

"So when do I have to clear out my desk?"

Wincing, the principal sighed. "Not till the semester ends in February. That'll give you plenty of time to send your résumé around."

It gave her four months, give or take a week. Dara sighed, staring out the window, where Old Glory popped and snapped in the brisk winter wind. She'd sat right here as a Centennial student when she'd served as an office aide to Mr. John Westfall, and again nearly nine years ago when he'd interviewed her to fill the open math teacher slot. There were other teaching positions available here in Howard County, and more than likely, she'd accept one. But it wouldn't be the same, because those schools wouldn't feel like *home*.

"Should I put in a good word for you over at River Hill?" Westfall asked, standing. "I hear there's going to be an opening there."

"Sure," Dara said, getting to her feet. "That'd be great."

"I hate to lose you, Dara. And so will the kids."

He extended his hand; she clasped it gratefully.

"It's gonna be like sending one of my own daughters off into—"

"Hush," she said, smiling sadly, "or you're going to make me cry."

"Don't want to start up any waterworks, now do we?"

Dara focused on their hands. He'd been jerking her arm up and down like a pump handle. "I've heard of trying to get blood from a turnip," she teased, "but I don't think this is the way you go about it."

Chuckling, Westfall let go of her hand, gave her shoulder a gentle squeeze. "If there's anything I can do,'' he said softly, "*anything*, you just ask, you hear?''

"Thanks,'' she said, heading for the door. "I will.''

"You'll come see me once in a while, won't you? Let me know how you're doing?''

Another nod, one hand on the doorknob. "Now, let me leave before I start blubbering all over this gorgeous green-and-orange carpet of yours!''

She closed his office door. Could things get any worse? she wondered. The second anniversary of her mother's death was just around the corner; in a week, her father would have been gone six months. Then there was the news about his so-called embezzlement. And now she was out of a job. If you had any sense, she said to herself, you'd make reservations and take that cruise you've been saving up for.

Immediately, she shook her head. No telling what Noah Lucas might do on Kurt Turner's behalf while you're off in the sunny Caribbean worrying yourself silly.

The janitor flung open the door, rolled his oversize metal trash can inside. As he banged and clanged down the hall, a huge gust of wind whipped in behind him, blowing the papers from Dara's hands and scattering them across the floor. Some fluttered out the door; others skidded under lockers. "That cruise is gone with the wind, too,'' she muttered as she gathered the papers that hadn't escaped.

Look at the bright side, she told herself. Now you have two projects to distract you from the Pinnacle mess—Sunday school and job hunting!

As she headed for her cubicle in the teachers' lounge, something told her neither would be a very good diversion....

* * *

The weather bureau was predicting snow. Lots of it. But it wasn't supposed to start until late afternoon, which meant Sunday services and Dara's class would take place as scheduled. If TV meteorologist Norm Lewis was right, there'd be no school tomorrow, and if her students had heard his report, they'd be too busy looking out the windows to learn much of anything this morning.

It was a good chance to put Naomi King's advice to the test: "You can't teach the little ones with ordinary lessons. If you follow the teacher's manual, they'll be bored and restless." The art project had worked quite well last week. Why not incorporate more of the same into this Sunday's lesson?

She'd purchased five jars of peanut butter, a bottle of vanilla, ten boxes of confectioners' sugar, two rolls of waxed paper, a monumental stack of foam bowls, three rolls of paper towels and a huge can of crushed peanuts at the grocery store yesterday. Dara could hear in their puzzled voices that she'd piqued her students' curiosity when she called each last evening and asked that they bring one of their fathers' old shirts to class, but it was nothing compared with the inquisitive looks on their faces when they marched into the room and saw the supplies, standing in a tidy row on her desk.

"I'll answer all your questions as soon as we've said our opening prayer," she promised. "Who'd like to do the honor?"

At first, Dara thought she might have to do it herself, as she had last week. Then one tiny hand slid hesitantly into the air.

"Thank you for volunteering, Bobby," she told him. "Now, let's all close our eyes and bow our heads."

The children immediately complied.

"Go ahead, Bobby."

"Dear Lord," he began in a sweet, angelic voice, "we thank You for getting us here safely. God bless Miss Mackenzie for being our teacher..." He hesitated for a moment before concluding. "And for bringing all the ingredients to make peanut butter balls. Amen."

"Peanut butter balls. What're peanut butter balls?"

The question echoed around the room a dozen times before Angie said, "They're a no-bake dessert that's very high in fat and—"

"But they're fun to make and dee-licious!" Bobby tacked on.

"How do you know 'bout peanut butter balls?" Pete asked.

"Our mother taught us to make them," was Angie's straightforward reply.

Dara clapped her hands. "All right, class, let's get our hands washed so we can dig in."

In a matter of minutes, they were back in their seats, draped in their fathers' baggy, cast-off shirts. "We're going to learn something about creation today," she said, going from desk to desk, rolling up sleeves. And handing each student a sheet of waxed paper, she added, "God took special ingredients, mixed them and made the world."

As Dara gave the children their own disposable bowls, she began quoting Genesis in words these first graders would understand. To emphasize the lesson, she doled out peanut butter and sugar, a drop of vanilla, and invited the kids to mix them thoroughly...with their bare hands. When they'd made dough of the mixture, she instructed them to form gumdrop-size balls from it, then instructed them to roll their peanut butter balls in the crushed nuts.

Lisa licked the mixture off her fingers. "Mmm," she said. "*That* was good work."

"And messy work," Tina agreed.

"But now we can enjoy—and share—what we've made," Dara told them.

"Oh, I get it!" Pete shouted. "Like God enjoyed the world, and shared it with Adam and Eve once he got done makin' it!"

"Once he had finished it," Angie corrected, sighing deeply.

"Is God gonna eat the world?" Donny teased, popping a peanut butter ball into his mouth.

"'Course not, stupid. It's too big to fit in His mouth," Pete said around a mouthful of his own sticky treat.

"It isn't polite to call people 'stupid,'" Angie scolded.

Dara had spent only two weeks with the class, but her students had spent three months with Angie. They rolled their eyes at her admonition.

Angie could pretend to be older and wiser than the rest of the kids in class, but Dara had seen her eyes light up at the prospect of digging her fingers into the gooey mess that would become the peanut butter balls. And despite her best attempts to appear above it all, her "cookies" were just as lopsided as everyone else's.

The children left class, chattering happily—around mouthfuls of the treat they'd made with their own two hands—about what they'd do once the snow started. Dara went about the business of cleaning up what Donny had referred to as "Our Genesis Mess."

Humming, she dropped sticky bowls and wrinkled

sheets of waxed paper into the wastebasket, then began packing up the leftover ingredients and paper products. Dara had but one regret about teaching this class: not one of the students was *her* son or daughter. She loved everything about children—from cradle to cap and gown—their effervescent exuberance to their bright-eyed view of the world was contagious. Someday, she hoped, the Lord would see fit to answer her prayer and send a good Christian man into her life.

One like Dad, she thought, gritting her teeth with grim determination. She would prove he hadn't committed that awful crime if it was the last thing she ever did!

He'd earned her faith in him, her loyalty, because he'd been a wonderful father, a wonderful husband! Dara recalled how well he'd always taken care of her mother, how much more devoted and compassionate he became when she got sick. Dara wanted a love like that, a man like that, with whom she could build a home, a family, a future—

"May I have a word with you, Miss Mackenzie?"

The suddenness of the deep baritone startled her, and Dara dropped the paper bag she'd been holding.

"Sorry," he said, a crooked smile slanting his tawny mustache, "didn't mean to frighten you."

She stooped to retrieve the paper towels and foam bowls that had rolled under her desk. "No problem. I just didn't see you there, that's all." Dara jammed the articles back into the bag, stood it near the door. "Now then," she said, dusting her hands in front of her, "what can I do for you, Mr. Lucas?"

He didn't answer right away, a fact that gave Dara an overall uneasy feeling. She was about to ask what he was looking at when he said, "I'd like to thank you."

"Thank me?" His intense scrutiny had unnerved her, and a jittery giggle popped from her lips. "Whatever for?"

"For attempting to comfort my daughter last week. Bobby told me what you said...and did."

Dara frowned, trying to remember specifically what he might be referring to. The hug? That little peck on the temple? She shrugged. "I'm afraid I don't—"

"I'm the one who's afraid, Miss Mackenzie," he interrupted. "Since my wife passed away, the children haven't had much in the way of female nurturing. I try," he added, shoulders up and palms extended, "but I make a better dad than a mom."

Dara took note of his broad shoulders, his muscular legs, the big fingers that repeatedly combed through his shining blond hair. I'll say, she thought, grinning inwardly. "Well, no one expects you to be a superhero," she said, "least of all, Bobby and Angie."

"Maybe not," he said in a quiet voice, "but they deserve the best, and I'm a far cry from it."

This was a side of Noah Lucas that Dara never would have guessed existed.

"I just wanted to thank you is all, for your kindness."

Coming from anyone else, the words would have been taken at face value, and she would have said, "Just doin' my job." But from a man like Noah Lucas—reserved, private, stoic—they took on a whole new meaning, because Dara had a feeling he didn't make a practice of saying such things.

"You can be very proud of Bobby and Angie," she admitted. "They are two of the best-behaved children

I've ever met." Grinning, she held a finger in the air to add, "And I'll have you know this isn't my first encounter with children."

"So I've heard."

So he *had* checked her out! The question was, had he done it because of the funny-money business down at Pinnacle? Or because she'd be spending an hour each week with his precious children? It had to be one or the other, because it was a sure bet he wasn't interested in her as a woman, Dara thought. More than likely, he believed that adage that the acorn didn't fall far from the tree, and intended to keep a very close eye on her for the duration of the Sunday-school class.

People are not what they appear to be.

If her father had said it once, he'd said it a hundred times. Where Noah Lucas was concerned, the statement seemed more prophetic than ever.

Had she misjudged him when she'd jumped to the conclusion that he was cold and heartless? Had she been wrong when she'd assumed Bobby and Angie behaved the way they did because he encouraged it?

"What was that, ah, that *stuff* they were eating when they walked out of here?" he asked, interrupting her reverie.

"Peanut butter balls."

"You taught them to make—"

She gave a proud nod. "Yup."

"How did you know it was safe?"

Dara tucked in one corner of her mouth. "Safe?"

"When I was a boy, I knew a girl who was allergic to peanuts. One whiff of anything made from them and she'd go into anaphylactic shock. More than once, she was carted off to the hospital in an ambulance, fighting for her life." He raised a brow. "I admire the extra effort it took on your part to ensure none of your students would have such a reaction.''

Was he…was he *smirking?*

Well, that sure isn't a smile on his face!

Noah Lucas had her dead to rights, and he knew it. She had made no such ''check'' to find out if any of the children might be allergic to peanuts, and the shame of it made her cheeks hot. It had been only by the grace of God that none of her first graders was allergic to peanuts. Later, she'd say a heartfelt prayer of thanks for the Almighty's protection. Right now, all Dara wanted to do was get rid of Noah Lucas.

She'd been right about him after all. He *was* a smug, patronizing know-it-all. And more than likely, he *had* been responsible for the way his children behaved. ''If there's nothing else, Mr. Lucas,'' she said, clipping her words, ''I have…I have a very busy day ahead of me.''

''Of course. Forgive me. It was never my intention to make you late for—'' the smirk became a grin ''—for your very busy day.''

Somehow, he knew full well that she had no plans for the rest of the day. But how could he have known? *Because he's researched you, that's how,* she reminded herself. She could hardly blame him; Dara had probed into his background, too. Straightening her back, she tilted her head. '' 'Know thine enemy,' eh, Mr. Lucas?''

That seemed to wipe the pompous look from his face!

''I'm sorry?''

Dara had no idea why the confusion that suddenly wrinkled his brow would make her feel the need to comfort and console him. But it did. Sighing with vexation, she put her back to him, pretending to be busy gathering her teacher's manual, her purse.

Lucas relieved her of the coat, held it out and waited for her to shrug into it. Funny, she thought, but I don't remember it feeling this heavy befo— Then she realized it had been his hands, resting on her shoulders, that had caused the added weight. Dara wondered how the touch of a man who had riled her temper in her father's office, who had further fueled her fury by pointing out that her inattentiveness might well have endangered an innocent child, would feel so comforting, so reassuring, so *right*.

Because, she decided, turning suddenly to face him, you're losing your mind. Nothing short of insanity, she believed, could explain why such a feeling would come over her.

"Angie and Bobby are waiting in the hall."

She raised a brow, as if to say, "What does that have to do with me?"

"They have something to ask you," Lucas said.

Dara glanced toward the door, and saw the children standing side by side. Lucas waved them in. "Go ahead," he encouraged, "you can ask her now."

Bobby took a half step forward. "Would you do us the honor of joining us for dinner?"

Chapter Two

Noah watched her face as a myriad of emotions—confusion, surprise, delight—flickered over her lovely features.

"Father is making lasagna," Bobby announced, nodding and grinning.

It was apparent that Noah's son wanted her to say yes every bit as much as he did.

Smiling, Dara lay a hand on the boy's shoulder. "My goodness! I don't know what to say."

"If you're busy," Angie said, "say no. If you're not…" The child held out her hands and lifted her shoulders.

Laughing softly, Dara combed her fingers through Angie's dark curls. Noah couldn't help but notice the way his little girl's too-old stare faded under Dara's tender touch. The children needed a woman like this…had *been* needing someone like Dara for nearly four years now.

The idea had begun to formulate last Sunday, when Bobby told him how Dara had hugged Angie in Sunday-school class and called her "sweetie" and referred to Francine as "Mommy." Since his wife's death, Noah had felt like a bumbling, stumbling mess when it came to providing affection. Oh, he doled out the occasional hug and kiss and greedily ate them up when the children offered them, but soft touches—like hair tousling and kisses—had not been a spontaneous part of his personality.

He could have blamed it on the fact that he'd been raised in an institutional setting with hundreds of parentless children just like him. He could have said it was because men weren't born with instinctive nurturing tendencies.

But neither was true, and Noah knew it.

The only person in the world he'd felt free to be completely open and honest with had been Francine. She'd seen the vulnerable, needy side of him—and had loved him in spite of it.

"I know you," she'd said days before her death. "You'll stick your nose in a ledger book and try to hide from the world." And grabbing a fistful of his shirt, she'd pulled him nearer with a strength that belied her condition. "The children will need you more than ever after I'm gone," she'd said. "Promise me you'll find a good woman who will be there for them. Someone who will make sure they get the guidance and discipline they need to become respectable citizens and obedient followers." She'd shaken a maternal finger under his nose to add, "She'll have to be a strong-willed woman who isn't afraid to speak her mind. You'll look for a woman like that, won't you, after I'm gone?"

Of course he'd promised. How could he have denied her at a time like that? It had been an easy enough vow to take; living up to it, he soon discovered, was what had required constant and serious effort.

Because he loved Angie and Bobby more than life itself. They were more than extensions of Francine and him, the children were proof of his love for her and hers for him. That love turned out to be a double-edged sword, for every time he looked into their sweet, angelic faces, he was reminded of that love, and missed it all the more.

They were such well-behaved children—everyone said so—never talking out of turn, always tidy and eager to please. In truth, Noah had no idea *why* they rarely cried or complained, why they never roughhoused like other children. He'd never asked perfection from them…

Had he?

So it was the most natural thing in the world, he decided, when Bobby told him how Dara had mothered Angie. Was it any surprise that the idea had begun to formulate?

"If you're busy," Angie was saying, "say no." If not, his daughter's dainty shrug implied, what else was there to say?

Dara met Noah's eyes, and the questions there made it clear she wasn't certain he'd approved the invitation.

"I make a mean Caesar salad," he prompted, "if I do say so myself."

"Wouldn't it be better to make a *nice* salad?" Angie asked, grinning.

"Nice is always better than mean," Dara teased, winking.

"Does that mean you're coming to dinner?" Bobby wanted to know.

Dara licked her lips. Swallowed. He could almost

see the wheels grinding in her head as she considered all the reasons she should say no. Then she focused a dark-eyed, loving gaze on his children, and he saw the indecision and apprehension disappear. In place of her wary smile there was a warm grin.

"I'll come," she told them, "but on one condition only."

Angie and Bobby probably didn't even realize they'd taken a step forward. Noah had felt the pull, too, but they were children, without a lifetime of restraint and self-control under their belts.

"What?" they asked.

"That you'll let me bring dessert."

The children exchanged a glance before facing her again. What happened next convinced Noah he'd made the right decision, that God had planted the idea in his head and would continue guiding his actions.

"Well, okay," Bobby began, slowly, quietly. Blue eyes alight with mischief, he added, "So long as it isn't…"

A moment of silence ticked by before Angie covered her mouth with both hands and giggled. He couldn't remember the last time his little girl had *acted* like a little girl. The sight touched him so much that Noah had to swallow to keep tears of gratitude at bay.

"Peanut butter balls!" she shouted through her fingers.

Dara got onto her knees, making herself child size, and held out her arms to them. The children melted against her like butter on a hot biscuit. That quickly, she'd worked her enchantment on them. "No peanut butter balls," she promised, smiling. "Now, tell me— what's your favorite dessert?"

"Brownies!" said Bobby.

"Chocolate cake!" Angie insisted.

Standing, Dara turned to Noah. "What time is dinner?" She spoke with the precise diction of a TV news anchor.

"Five o'clock?"

When she nodded, her shining reddish brown curls bounced. "Is your place easy to find?"

He never went anywhere without his trusty pen and pencil. Can't tell when you might need to work out a problem, he'd found. He flipped open the pad, quickly jotted down the directions, then placed the small sheet of paper into her palm, closing his large hand around hers. "Route 40 west," he said, pretending not to notice the slight tremor, "left on Centennial Lane, right at the light at Old Annapolis. We're the fourth house on the right." He turned her loose. "You can't miss us."

She stared at the directions, then looked at him. In school, when the teachers weren't watching, he'd made fun of the supersensitive male poets who'd written lush prose describing how it felt to be lost in a woman's gaze. He hadn't understood a word of their sweet talk, because frankly, he couldn't get a handle on the *why* of it.

He understood them now, as he looked into dusky eyes that made Dara seem mysterious and elusive and at the same time vulnerable and sensitive, with a capacity for love like no one he'd ever known.

It disappointed him more than he cared to admit when she blinked, turned that warmth on his children again. "See you in a few hours, then," Dara said, waving and smiling as he took them by the hand and led them toward the big double doors at the end of the hall. Bobby and Angie turned three, perhaps four times to look over their shoulders, tripping over his feet and their own before he was able to guide them outside.

Clearly, his children were charmed by Dara Mackenzie.

He had a feeling it was going to take a concerted effort on his part to keep her charm from working on *him*.

The kids had been in the living room for half an hour already, knobby knees poking into the cushions, elbows resting on the sofa back as they pressed their noses to the windowpane. "Where *is* she?" Angie sighed.

Chuckling, Noah said, "It's only four-thirty, sweet girl. Miss Mackenzie said she'd be here a little before five, remember?"

"But it's snowing harder now. Do you think she decided not to come?"

"I think she would have called."

"But maybe *you* should call and offer to pick her up and bring her here, Father."

"Maybe."

"I saw one car slipping and sliding a few minutes ago. Do you think she was in an accident?"

It surprised him, the way his heartbeat quickened at the possibility. "I'm sure she'll be here any minute, Angie." But Noah sent a prayer heavenward on Dara's behalf, just in case....

"Do you think she's..." Bobby squinted, searching his memory for the right word. "Do you think Miss Mackenzie is a *punk*-shal kind of person?"

"Yes, she seems the punctual type."

"I hope she doesn't get lost."

"She won't," Angie confidently assured him.

Noah pocketed his hands and leaned on the door frame as he watched them, heads turning to follow every car that drove up or down the street. He couldn't remember the last time he'd seen them looking forward to having a guest to dinner. Fact was, he'd *never* seen them so excited about company, particularly female company.

A year or so ago, he'd warily ventured back into the dating scene, but only because his wife had insisted that he try, as soon as possible, to find a mother substitute for Angie and Bobby. He might not have considered it even then if Bobby hadn't asked, "Father, do you ever get lonely?"

The answer had cried out from his heart, from his head. Yes! he'd wanted to shout, yes, I'm lonely. He'd felt the pangs of it day and night, starting on the morning when Francine's doctor had announced her prognosis. But he couldn't very well admit it to the boy. The children needed his strength, not his weakness. So he'd said, "Now, why would I be lonesome when I have you and your sister to keep me company?"

Either Bobby hadn't heard him, or chose to ignore the comment. "I get sad sometimes," Bobby had said, "because I miss Mother."

Angie, he recalled, had not agreed. He'd sloughed it off to immaturity; perhaps the girl felt her mother had abandoned them.

"No need to be sad, kids," he'd said, "because your mother is in heaven now, with Jesus."

"Is she happy there?" Angie had wanted to know.

Francine had talked so much about paradise in those last, pain-filled days. "Yes, I believe she is."

Bobby nodded. "Do you think she misses us?"

He'd looked into his little boy's face, a face so small,

so innocent, yet so old and wise. "Of course she does. Your mother loved you more than...more than life itself."

Angie had sighed heavily and frowned. "Then I don't see how she can be happy." She'd met Noah's eyes and said very matter-of-factly, "I'm sure not happy when I think about how much I miss *her*."

They'd been so young when Francine died—Angie, four and Bobby three—too young to remember much about their mother. Or so the experts said.

"They miss the things she did for them," insisted the Christian counselor Noah had hired. "Have you considered remarrying, Mr. Lucas?"

In truth, he had not. It may not be macho to admit it in this day and age, but Noah had never been with any woman except Francine. The thought of sharing himself so completely with another woman...

But the therapist's words had echoed Francine's own. If it would help his children, he'd set aside his feelings, take another wife. But it would have to be in name only, he told himself time and again, because the woman hadn't been born who could replace Francine in his heart.

He'd learned to trust his children's instincts about potential dates. They liked Dara Mackenzie. Noah had a feeling that tonight's dinner was going to end up quite differently.

"Father, she's here!" Angie announced, in a voice filled with anticipation and wonder.

Chapter Three

"I'll wash, you dry," Dara suggested as she stacked the dinner plates, "since you know where everything goes."

He gave her a sideways look. "I realize I come off as an old-fashioned stick-in-the-mud kind of guy," he said, "but a couple of years back, I actually invested in a modern-day gizmo called a dishwasher."

Dara grinned as Noah carried the nearly empty lasagna tray to the sink. "Amazing contraption," he continued. "Put the dirty dishes in, close the door, and voilà! Clean dishes!"

"I stand corrected, Mr. Lucas."

"'Noah,' Miss Mackenzie."

"'Dara,' Mr. Lucas."

He chuckled, tore off a sheet of aluminum foil and covered the leftover lasagna. "We could go on this way long into the night."

"I'm afraid I can't stay long into the night. In fact," she said, standing on tiptoe at the window, "I should probably have left half an hour ago. I imagine the snow has started to mount up by now.''

Noah flipped a switch near the back door, flooding the yard with light.

Dara gasped. ''Oh, my goodness! It's white, as far as the eye can see, and still coming down like crazy.'' She glanced at Noah, who had parted the miniblinds to stare out the half window in the back door. ''How deep do you think it is?''

He squinted into the snowy night. ''The bottom step is completely buried, and the snow is halfway up the second.'' He met her eyes. ''If I had to guess, I'd say there's more than a foot.'' He snapped the blinds shut. ''We could get another twelve inches before it's over.''

''But it's not even Thanksgiving yet!'' Dara glanced at the wall clock, then gasped. ''How could it be nearly nine o'clock already!''

Noah shrugged. ''Time sure flies when you're having fun?''

''I suppose,'' she said distractedly, looking out the window again. ''I hope they've plowed the roads. I don't know if my car will make it through a foot of snow otherwise.''

He held out his hand. ''Let's take a gander out the front window and see if the plows have been by or not.''

Hesitantly, she put her hand into his and let him lead her down the hall and into the living room. Had she done or said something to make him think she'd accepted his invitation because she was *interested* in him? The last thing on her mind had been romance!

Well, not the *last* thing, but romance certainly hadn't been the primary reason for the visit. Her plan had been simple and straightforward: hire Noah Lucas to help her prove that her father had not committed a crime. She hadn't expected to have an opportunity to discuss the arrangement this evening, what with the children around, but she *had* presumed the dinner would be a good start, a place to establish the rapport required to make the question possible…later.

Dara didn't know if she'd define what they'd established tonight as "rapport," but *something* had developed between them, or that almost kiss wouldn't have happened in the kitchen earlier.

She blamed it on tension, hers *and* Noah's. He hadn't so much as hinted at that distasteful Pinnacle matter, to give him his due, but it was there anyway, like a translucent fog. Her nerves had been in a knot since he'd first told her about the charges against her father. Surely it was on Noah's mind, too, since he'd have to be the one to start the prosecution ball rolling.

"I thought you might like the opportunity to replace the money," Noah had offered, even before she'd taken a seat that first day, "before I make my report to Kurt Turner, if I can legitimately attest that the funds are here…"

Dara had a respectable sum piled up in her savings account, and she'd invested a few dollars in the stock market, as well. But two hundred thousand?

He'd been reserved, businesslike, coldly calculating up until that point, but the moment she admitted she couldn't put her hands on that kind of money, his demeanor changed. His frown had deepened, and he dug into the file as if he'd gone back a hundred years in time, to some dusty Texas town where a rustler had escaped the jailer's wagon. In a snap, it was as though he saw himself headin' up the posse that would hunt down the bad guy, then hold him till the sheriff showed up to haul the varmint off to the hoosegow.

She could tell by the way he attacked this case that he could be as determined as a bloodhound, as ruthless as a pit bull. If she could harness that tenacity, put it to work *on her father's behalf*...

"How can I get you on *my* side?" she intended to ask. Cut and dried. Period. From what little she knew of him, a man like that would probably admire her straightforwardness, because she'd be speaking *his* language.

A man like *what?*

He wasn't cold and heartless. At least, not entirely. He was strict with the children, but what choice did he have, when circumstances had forced him to be both mother and father to them?

He was still holding her hand when they walked into his living room, where the children lay on their stomachs, chins propped in upturned palms, staring at the TV.

"What are you watching?" Noah asked.

"Some show about angels." Angie rolled over to face her father. "See that man with the long blond hair?"

He nodded.

"He's one of the angels. Can you believe it? I didn't know there were such things as *boy* angels."

Chuckling, Noah said, "Some of the most powerful angels in God's kingdom were *boys*. There was the archangel Gabriel, remember, and Michael, and—"

"Boat angels are no big deal," Bobby said.

"Boat angels?" Dara asked.

Sitting cross-legged, the boy faced her. "You know, like the ones on the ark?"

Dara smiled. "*Ark*-angels. Of course." And laughing, she said, "*You're* an angel. A nutty one."

The show's credits scrolled up the screen as Noah said, "It's after nine, kids. Time for bed."

"But there won't be any school tomorrow, Father. The weatherman said so, because of all the snow outside."

"You're probably right, Angie, but you've both been up since six." He smiled. "Now, say good-night to Miss Mackenzie and run upstairs. I'll be up in a minute to tuck you in and hear your prayers."

Without another word of protest, the children turned off the TV.

"Thank you for the dessert, Miss Mackenzie," Bobby said.

Angie nodded. "It was delicious."

Dara laid her hands on their shoulders. "I had a wonderful time. And to prove it, maybe I'll teach you to make ice-cream-cone cakes sometime soon."

Cheery faces tilted up to meet her eyes. "Really? When?"

"We'll discuss it in the morning," Noah interrupted gently. "Now, scoot! Call me when you've changed into your pajamas."

Dara opened the front door a crack, peeked out into the snowy night. "Hmm...the plows haven't been by yet." She stood for a moment, transfixed by the sight. "It's so beautiful out there," she whispered, hugging herself to fend off the chill, "all hushed and white and sparkly."

Noah rested his chin on her shoulder to have a look for himself. "Beautiful," he agreed.

He was behind her, so she couldn't read the expression that accompanied the unadorned statement, yet something in his full, rich baritone told Dara he wasn't referring to the wintry landscape. The shiver that ran through her had nothing to do with the temperature, because there he was again, unsettlingly close.

"I'd better be going," she said, trying to hide the tremor in her voice, "before it gets any worse."

"Before what gets worse?"

Swallowing a gasp, she gave a thought to the possibility that he could read her mind. Then, dismissing it, she said, "The weather, of course."

Noah turned her to face him. "You can't drive that puddle jumper of yours in this mess." With his free hand, he closed the door. "First snowplow that comes along will bury you for sure."

"Well, I can't stay *here*. What would people think?"

"They'd think you were smart enough to know better than to risk your life to protect your reputation."

Reputation. The word reverberated in her ears. Preserving her father's reputation had been the sole reason she'd come here.

Or had it?

Whatever the reason, it had gotten lost amid the children's happy banter, a home-cooked meal, a near kiss....

Now I know why they say you can't judge a book by its cover. Noah had all but destroyed her original assessment of him with the affection he'd showered on his kids, with the home he'd made for them. If only he had been the brutal businessman she'd thought him to be, Dara wouldn't be fighting her feelings for him now!

And how do you feel about him?

The answer was easy: she liked him. Liked him a great deal. Which made things hard, very hard, because in order for her plan to work, she would have to keep things "strictly business."

Wouldn't she?

Dara had heard of being backed into a corner, but it had never actually happened to her before. Well, you're cornered now, she told herself, figuratively and literally. She stood, shoulders and backside pressed against the cool wall, blinking into his dark-lashed blue eyes. Instinct told her Noah would never harm her. So what're you afraid of? she wondered as her heartbeat doubled.

Was fear responsible for her racing pulse? Or had some other emotion made her feel light-headed and jittery, like a girl in the throes of her first crush?

The only light in the foyer spilled in from the living room, soft and dim and puddling on the deep-green slate in buttery pools. The hazy amber rays painted his face in light and shadow, accenting the patrician nose, the square jaw, the fullness of his thickly mustached mouth.

She wasn't afraid of *him*, Dara realized. Rather, it was her *reaction* to him that scared her witless. The pull couldn't have been stronger, not if he were made of ore and a magnet had been implanted in her heart.

Noah pressed his palms against the wall, one on either side of her head. "If you insist on going home," he said, "I insist on driving you."

"But…"

But that would mean bundling the children up and loading them into the car, putting all three Lucases at risk on the slick, snow-covered roads.

"But what?" Noah asked.

Dara closed her eyes. *Lord*, she prayed, *tell me what to do!*

"Father," Angie called from the top of the stairs, "we're ready."

"I'll be right there."

His mustache grazed her cheek before he pulled away. Without taking his gaze from Dara's eyes, he grabbed her hand, led her back into the kitchen. "There's a canister of hot chocolate in the pantry. Why don't you fix us both a cup while I make my rounds."

She glanced toward the French doors that led to the deck. Noah hadn't turned off the spotlights, and they illuminated thousands of fat snowflakes, as big as quarters, that drifted down and landed silently atop the high, silvery drifts. Every twig and branch seemed to reach up and out, welcoming the thick downy blanket of white. Lovely as it was, Dara couldn't drive in this. Noah had been right: her aging little compact could barely make it over speed bumps; it would never make it through a foot and a half of heavy, wet snow.

One foot on the bottom step, he turned and said, "I think the snow is a blessing in disguise."

"A blessing?"

He nodded. "There's something I've been meaning to talk to you about, and now that you're a captive audience…" He gave her a small, mysterious smile, then climbed the stairs two at a time.

Does he want to talk more about the Pinnacle funds? Dara wondered as he disappeared around the landing. She had the impression that subject was talked through. Shrugging, she walked into the kitchen. After filling the gleaming chrome teapot with tap water and setting it atop the back burner, Dara grabbed two mugs from the cabinet above the dishwasher. *He doesn't seem like the cocoa type to me,* she told herself, dropping a tea bag into each cup. And while she waited for the water to boil, Dara wandered into the family room, where she held her hands above the warmth radiating from the big black woodstove.

She'd heard that Noah had lost his wife several years before moving here. So who had decorated this room? The furniture looked brand-new. Twin muted-blue plaid sofas, facing each other, flanked the fireplace. At either end of each stood a bleached-oak table. On one sat a lamp made from a birdhouse; on another, a brass lantern that had the earmarks of an antique. Magazines, arranged in a fan shape, lay on the coffee table. And framed photographs, rather than paintings or prints, decorated the walls.

Dara moved in for a closer look, saw first a five-by-seven picture of Angie, bundled in a bunting, snuggled in her mother's arms. Noah's wife had been a beauty, just as Dara had suspected. Long, dark hair spilled over one shoulder, and wide, brown eyes gleamed with maternal pride as she smiled at her infant daughter. Another picture, taken a year later, showed her in a similar pose, this time with Bobby on her lap.

Beside that photograph hung an eight-by-ten full-color portrait of Noah and Francine on their wedding day. Her shimmering hair had been gathered in a loose topknot and secured by a wreath of tiny red roses and baby's breath. The off-the-shoulder gown skimmed her trim waist and hips, rippled out behind her like a white satin river. And Noah, outfitted like royalty in a white tuxedo, stood straight backed and beaming beside his beautiful new wife.

Like the stage manager of a one-act play, the photographer had set the scene, positioning the bride and groom face-to-face on the altar's red-carpeted steps, arranging her gauzy veil to float around her face like a translucent cloud. He'd placed vases of flowers at their feet, linked their hands around the stems of her red-rose bouquet. Talent and artistry aside, he could not have fabricated the love that blazed in their eyes.

Dara had dreamed all her life of loving—of being loved—like that. What would it be like to have found and lost it, as Noah so obviously had? Devastating, she thought. And for the first time since their meeting, Dara believed she understood why Noah sometimes seemed so standoffish, indifferent, almost harsh with his children: he was holding life at arm's length to protect himself from experiencing such pain ever again.

But if that was the case, why had he come so close to kissing her…not once but twice!

Sighing, Dara returned to the kitchen, where the water was at a full boil in the kettle. How would Noah take his tea? she asked herself, stirring half a teaspoon of sugar into her own mug. With honey and lemon? Cream and sugar? Or just plain? If she had to guess, she'd choose the latter. Everything else about him was no-frills, from the neatly trimmed mustache above his upper lip to the gleam of his razor-cut hair.

And whatever it was that he wanted to say to her, she had a feeling he'd get straight to the point.

Francine had always been the one who'd listened to their prayers, but once she accepted the fact that her illness was terminal, she had said, "It's important that you be there for them, morning and night. How else will they learn that talking to God can be as easy and as natural as breathing?"

It had been just one of the many things he'd promised in her last hours. So far, he hadn't let her down. With the help of a cleaning service, he kept the house shipshape and saw to it Angie and Bobby ate three squares a day. He made sure they continued with their piano lessons and took her place in helping them with their homework. And most important of all, he'd made a point of attending Sunday services with them after their Bible class ended. "Children learn by example," Francine had said.

More times than he cared to admit, Noah wished he'd been more observant of all the little things she'd done to make his life pleasant and peaceful. Things like pretty flower arrangements that brightened dark corners. His bathrobe, belted and hanging neatly in their closet. Socks, freshly laundered and paired, then rolled into a ball and tucked into his top dresser drawer.

She'd known without his saying so that he didn't like his feet cramped into a tightly sheeted bed. And so, in addition to covers that were pulled back and smoothed, Francine had, without fail, *un*tucked the sheets and blankets every night.

Raised in St. Vincent's Orphanage with nothing but a change of clothes to call his own, the closest he'd come to loving and being loved was when old Brother Constantine invited the lonely boy to join him for his daily walks around the academy grounds.

He'd been dumped on the headmaster's doorstep at the tender age of two, and by the time Noah turned fourteen, he'd given up hope that one of the smiling couples who came "visiting" would take *him* home. The starry-eyed ladies and their stoic husbands were looking for babies, after all, and he'd grown too tall, too gangly, for their tastes. Besides, if his own mother hadn't wanted him, why should anyone else?

But years of the brother's quiet and steadfast acceptance opened the boy's heart to the possibility, at least, that one day he might find the kind of warmth that can be generated only by a loving family. And when he was twenty-two, four full years after he'd left St. Vincent's and Brother Constantine behind, Noah found it in the arms of Francine Brewster.

Her motherly ministrations were like soothing salve, healing the raw wounds of desperation inflicted by years of believing love was an emotion intended for everyone, anyone but him.

He had accepted her gift of unconditional love, and, believing it was far better to *show* her that he appreciated it, Noah took to doing little things for his wife. Things like surprising her with bouquets of wildflowers, plucked from the roadside; building a potting shed out back, complete with heat and electricity, where she could tend her green-leafed "pets." He added a room to the back of their Pennsylvania farmhouse so she'd have a place to read when the mood struck.

Oh, how she'd brightened his life! Noah often said he would have tried to reel in the sun if she thought it might warm her, would have gathered up the stars to add sparkle to her life. She'd laugh softly and wave his wishes away, saying, "You're plenty warm and sparkly for me!"

Still, he'd have done anything she'd asked of him, because Noah believed that *nothing* he did or built or said could ever balance the scales once she'd given him those precious treasures called Angela Marie and Robert Edward.

He missed her. Missed the companionship and the camaraderie. And being with Dara tonight had reminded him that a rock-solid marriage could be as comfortable as a feather bed.

He hadn't met a person who didn't love Dara—and

he'd spoken to dozens in trying to find out if she might be involved in the embezzlement scheme. Why, he'd need a calculator to count up all the people who said she'd done them a favor or a kindness over the years!

She certainly had a way with children, his own in particular. She had an incredible sense of humor. And from all he'd seen, she enjoyed hard work. He sensed that the sweetness in her started in her heart, reverberated to every other part of her. And she's certainly pretty enough, he thought, picturing her dark doe eyes, her bouncy curls, her heart-stopping smile.

More importantly, Dara was a devout follower. That was essential. Francine had specifically told him if love ever came knocking again, he should open the door—provided a Christian woman stood on the other side. "A believer will see to it Angie and Bobby are raised in the faith. She'll teach them through her own example, not just by words alone."

He'd prayed himself hoarse over it; if he had to re-hitch his wagon—and according to the counselor, that's exactly what his kids needed most right now—why not yoke himself to someone he sincerely respected, a woman he genuinely *liked?*

Noah shrugged. Because who knows? You might just find yourself feeling more than friendship for Dara...one day.

If he was honest with himself, he'd have to admit he felt more than that for her *now*. How else was he to explain the way his heart had thundered when he'd *almost* held her in his arms...when he'd *almost* kissed her lovely pink lips....

"Father?" Angela Marie was saying now.

She'd caught him daydreaming, and she knew it. Noah returned her mischievous smile.

"Good thing you listened to my prayers *last*," she said, grinning.

He tucked the covers up under her chin. "And why is that?"

"Because Bobby gets his feelings hurt if you don't pay attention to *his* prayers, remember?"

Nodding, Noah chuckled. "What makes you think I wasn't paying attention to your prayers?"

"Because," she said matter-of-factly, "you didn't say 'Amen' when I finished."

"Good night, sweet girl," he said, bending to kiss her forehead.

He turned out the light, and as he stepped into the hall, he heard her whisper, "I love you, Father."

"I love you, too."

Heart knocking against his ribs, he descended the stairs and headed for the kitchen, where Dara was waiting for him. What he was about to say wouldn't be easy, but it would be right.

Dara had finished one cup of tea and was halfway through a second before she decided to wait for him in the family room, where it was warmer. According to the carriage clock on top of the TV, he'd been gone twenty minutes.

It seemed like an hour.

Dara worried about staying the night. What would his neighbors say when the little red car that had been parked in his driveway before the snow started was still there in the morning? What would Angie and Bobby think when they woke up and found their Sunday-school teacher asleep on the sofa in their family room? And speaking of Sunday school, how would the parents of her other students feel when they found out she'd spent the night in a widower's house?

You're a grown-up, they'd scold, why didn't you check the weather before it got too hazardous to drive? To which she'd reply, Well, if they don't think any better of me than that...

Still, others might say that she'd subconsciously allowed herself to get waylaid at Noah's house. Some would no doubt think it hadn't been unconscious at all, that she'd deliberately gotten stranded, miles from home, on one of the worst weather nights of the year.

Dara sighed. Because, in all honesty she didn't know which scenario was true.

She was standing at the stove when she heard him coming down the hall. "How do you take your tea?" she asked when he came in from the small home office adjacent to the kitchen.

He carried a thick accordion file under his arm. "No hot chocolate?"

"I figured you'd suggested it only on my behalf."

Grinning, he said, "You figured right."

"So...?" She pointed to the mug

He hesitated a moment before saying, "Strong and black."

She wondered about the tick in time that had passed before he answered. But his response had been what she'd expected: no frills, just like Noah himself.

"Sorry it took so long up there. The kids get a little wordy sometimes."

It isn't like I was going anywhere, she wanted to say, not with a foot and a half of snow on the ground. "I didn't mind," she said, instead. "I made myself comfortable in the family room. It's very warm and cozy in there."

"Then what say we bring the—" He frowned at the file. "How about if we drink our tea in the family room?"

The way he'd stopped midsentence Dara knew he hadn't said what he'd intended. His serious expression told her it wouldn't be long until he did.

She carried their mugs into the family room. While she'd waited for him to tuck the children in, Dara had decided the big overstuffed recliner in the corner was Noah's. Her father had had a favorite chair, and it, too, had that certain comfortably worn quality. She put one mug on the table beside it, placed the other on the coffee table and nodded at the file. "What's that?" she asked, sitting on the end of the couch nearest his chair.

"Something I've been meaning to talk to you about," he said, sliding a manila folder from the file. "But before I show you what's in here, I want you to know I feel terrible about this."

Why did his tone of voice, his choice of words, remind her of when her father used to begin her childhood scoldings with "This is going to hurt me more than it hurts you"?

"I gave a lot of thought to what you'd said the other day in your father's office, that he wasn't the kind of man who could steal."

Dara's heart hammered; her palms grew moist. This was going to be much more serious than any reprimand her dad had ever doled out.

"I never had the pleasure of meeting him," Noah continued, "but his reputation as an honest businessman was well-known…and well-deserved, from everything I've heard. That's what prompted me to take another look into this matter of…of embezzlement."

Embezzlement. The word echoed loudly, harshly, in

her ears, like the deep, repeating grate of the school's fire alarm.

"You sounded so sure of his innocence," Noah said, "that it made me believe if I dug deep enough, looked long enough, I might just find the proof you were talking about, proof that would clear his name."

"You're not going to believe this, but…"

"But what?"

"I came here tonight hoping to discuss that very thing with you."

His furrowed brow told her he still didn't understand.

"I was hoping you'd go to work for *me*, looking for…looking for—"

"Proof that would clear your father's name?" he repeated.

Dara nodded. "You didn't find it, did you?"

His somber expression was her answer.

Noah took a deep breath, handed Dara the file. "I didn't leave a stone unturned. I checked into everything. No one escaped my scrutiny, not the board of directors, not Kurt Turner, not the bookkeeper or even the secretary." Noah paused, still frowning. "Only a handful of people had access to that money, and each one of them could account for every cent." He met her eyes, his frown intensifying slightly. "The trail dead-ends at your father's door."

He had nothing to gain by lying to her, Dara realized. In fact, his stellar reputation could only improve if he managed to turn up documentation that cleared her father's name. She opened the file, flipped nervously through the paperwork inside. But she couldn't read what was printed on the pages, because Dara couldn't see through her tears.

Right from the start, something had told her things might turn out this way. She'd hoped and prayed for a different ending, of course, an ending that would show the Kurt Turners of the world that, despite his unconventional behavior, Jake Mackenzie had been a good and decent man.

He'd always been eccentric, a bit offbeat. But *that* had been what set him apart from the crowd; his business successes had been a direct result of what some called "personality quirks" and "peculiarities." Everyone said so, including her father!

It had never taken much to satisfy him. "Three square meals and a cot," he'd often say, "and I'm a happy man." Then, with no warning whatever, the simple life no longer seemed to satisfy him. He started jetting all over the country, "lunching" with big shots from Johns Hopkins and the National Institutes of Health, saying only that his meetings with the top docs would improve life for everybody.

His actions grew more and more unpredictable, especially those months before the first heart attack. And in the weeks before he'd left for England, Dara's gregarious, easygoing, amiable father became elusive, secretive, overly sensitive to questions.

All right. So he had taken the money. But why, she wondered. *"Why?"*

Noah sat beside her on the sofa, slipped an arm around her shoulders. He handed her his handkerchief.

She sniffed. "I'm sorry. I don't mean to be such a ba—"

"No need for tears *or* apologies." He kissed her temple. "Because I have an idea that I think will right all the wrongs in both our lives."

Dara dabbed at her eyes. "I don't see how that's

possible,'' she said, smiling, ''but you've sure got my attention.''

He turned her to face him, rested his hands on her shoulders, his intense gaze stealing her breath away.

''Marry me.''

Chapter Four

Surely she hadn't heard him correctly...he hadn't really asked her to marry him.

Had he?

Dara blinked the last of her tears away. "I, ah, I'm sorry, Noah. My pity party must have affected my hearing."

"You heard me right."

She stiffened as he plunged on.

"See, it's like this. Pinnacle hired me to find that money. They don't care *where* I find it, so if I find it in my own account—"

"*Your* account?" She pressed her fingertips against her temples and squinted. "I'm afraid I'm not following you," she said, shaking her head. "This is a lot to absorb in just a few minutes. I mean...I just found out my father is a...a criminal, and then I get...I get proposed to by a man I barely know." She shook her head again. "Wait a minute. You said they wouldn't care if you found the missing money in your account. How did it get into your account, anyway?"

"I never said it *was* in my account. What I said was, I'd replace it with my own two hundred thousand. Of course, I'll have to let that account go. It would be a conflict of interest to work on Pinnacle if we were married."

She took a deep breath, let it out slowly. "So you're saying…" Frowning, Dara met his eyes. He'd said it straight out: "Dara, will you marry me?" But why would he say such a thing? And what did it have to do with the missing money?

Dara was beginning to get a headache. "Exactly what *are* you saying?"

"Look, it's simple. I happen to know that you'll be out of a job in a few months, and I figure money's gonna be scarce, so—"

Dad is guilty, she thought, barely hearing a word Noah was saying. She didn't want to believe it, but she had a lapful of evidence that said otherwise. But wait— had she heard right? Had Noah said something about her losing her job? "How do you know I'll soon be out of work? I only found out myse—"

Staring at the toes of his sneakers, he tucked in one corner of his mouth. "I just know, okay?" And before she had a chance to ask how, he met her eyes. "You know as well as I do that Angie and Bobby need a mother. And I know as well as you do that your father's reputation is important to you. Very important." He shrugged. "So, what I'm proposing is this. I'll put the money back…if you'll become my wife."

Dara could only stare at him in silent disbelief. "You…you want to *buy* me?"

"Of course not," he snapped.

"Well, what would *you* call it?" Not ten minutes had passed since he'd handed her proof positive that

her father—the man she had always thought could do
no wrong—was a fraud. Jake Mackenzie had been her
protector, her provider, her *hero*, for goodness' sake,
for thirty years. If *he* had feet of clay...

"No one will ever have to know about what happened at Pinnacle," he was saying.

What had happened at Pinnacle in and of itself
would have been more than enough to stagger her. She
wouldn't have thought it possible to top the news, and
then Noah had pitched his either-or proposition.

Some choice! she thought. Marry Noah, and Dad's
reputation as an honest businessman stands, or... She
pictured the plaque on the office wall, commissioned
by the men and women who had worked for Jake Mackenzie. Friend and Father to Us All, it said. What
would they think of their "friend and father" if they
knew he'd stolen company funds for—

What did you do with that money, Dad? she demanded. Perhaps if she knew the answer to that, she'd
understand *why* he'd done something so out of char-
acter in the first place. You're grasping at straws, she
thought, cupping her elbows. You want easy answers,
and there are none.

Dara began to pace as a plethora of thoughts flitted
through her head, among them, that her fondest childhood dream had turned into a nightmare. She hadn't
even gone to kindergarten yet when she began believing in the beautiful fairy tale—a handsome prince
would carry her off on his white steed to a life of picket
fences and the pitter-patter of little feet. But if Jake
Mackenzie—whom she'd admired all her life—could
do something so underhanded, it could only mean one
thing: her handsome prince wasn't coming, because no
such man existed.

She heaved a sad sigh and glanced around Noah's family room, at the tidy furnishings, the ceiling-to-floor flagstone behind the woodstove where the family photographs hung. Why hadn't she noticed it before? There wasn't a knickknack or collectible in sight. No throw pillows on the couch, no scatter rugs underfoot. *I've seen homier rooms in furniture advertisements.*

And then it struck her. That was what Noah was looking for...someone to give this place a woman's touch. She frowned, staring at the nubby texture of the beige carpeting beneath her feet. *Why doesn't he just hire somebody? It sure would be easier.*

She stood at the French doors, staring out across the frosty expanse of lawn. Pressing her forehead against the smooth, cool glass, she closed her eyes. "I don't think you really want to saddle yourself with a wife, Noah," she said softly. Straightening, Dara drew a frowny face in the vapor her breath had created on a windowpane. "You want a nanny. A housekeeper. *Both,* maybe." She tucked her hand into her sleeve, wiped the smile away. "The Yellow Pages are full—"

"Been there, done that," came his brusque interruption.

She turned in time to see him run both hands through his hair.

"Look, I've had it up to here," he steamed, stroking a fingertip across his throat, "with women who're content to put in a nine-to-five day, who'll do only what's absolutely necessary to earn their paychecks and not one whit more. My kids need more than a clean house and well-balanced meals. They need..."

He clamped his teeth together, lips and eyes narrowing in frustration. "I'll tell you what I want, Dara." He stood between the coffee table and the sofa, feet planted shoulder-width apart, and jabbed the air with a forefinger. "What I want is someone who will love my kids as if they were her own, someone who'll genuinely care about every minute detail of their lives—from what they wear to bed to who they choose as playmates to whether or not they say their prayers." He threw both hands into the air. "If I had access to all the money in the world, I couldn't buy that!"

Dara's eyes widened with surprise at the ferocity in his quietly faltering voice. He closed his eyes, as if to summon self-control, and, chin resting on his chest, whispered, "I *know* you'd be good for Angie and Bobby."

"Two hundred thousand dollars' worth?" she snapped.

Crossing the room in three long strides, he grasped her hands, gave them a gentle squeeze. "It's a win-win situation, as I see it."

"That's not the way *I* see it! If I marry you, my father gets his good name back, you get a chief cook and bottle washer and your kids get a substitute mother." She paused, lower lip trembling with frustration. "What's in it for *me?*"

He blinked. Licked his lips. "I—I, ah, I guess I never looked at it that way."

She snatched back her hands, folded them tightly in front of her and shot a furtive glance at the doorway. If only she could leave, right now!

Dara stared outside, where the snow was falling harder than ever. It was everywhere now, two feet deep and mounting steadily; clinging to tree limbs, hugging the twigs of shrubs and bushes; blanketing the wrought-iron deck furniture; burying flower beds. When she'd peeked out the front door earlier, it had climbed halfway up the tires of her car. It was sure to have hidden them by now. Escape was impossible; she was trapped.

She heard him quietly step up behind her. Inhaling the faint masculine scent of his woodsy aftershave, she felt the heat and weight of his hands on her shoulders.

"We have an awful lot in common, you and I," he whispered into her ear.

"Like what!"

"We get along pretty well, and you seemed to like my cooking," he joked. "And I can see it in your eyes when you look at Angie and Bobby—you really care about them."

"Well, of course I do. A person would need a heart made of wood not to care about those—"

"Then give me one good reason we shouldn't get married."

There were a whole *host* of reasons—not the least of which was that they'd only just met—but the most important reason screamed in her head. "Because we don't love each other," she said. Surely he couldn't argue with *that*.

The sandy brows drew together as his lips tightened beneath the tawny mustache. Like a swift punch to the jaw, Dara's straightforward remark seemed to have caught him off guard, as if he'd expected her to smile and pull out her pocket calendar, start talking dates and gowns and—

"It's been my experience that good marriages have to be built on a stronger foundation than love alone," he said. "If they're to endure the test of time, they'd better be made of sturdier stuff—more dependable stuff—than—"

"But without love," she interrupted, "your so-called

strong foundation might as well be sand. You ought to know that better than most, since your marriage to Francine was so…so *perfect*.''

Dara blamed her terse comment on having just discovered that everything she'd believed all her life about her father was a lie. On feeling cornered by Noah, his proposal. On the weather. The late hour. She pressed her fingertips into her eyes.

"Hey," he said softly, "don't cry."

"Give me one good reason," she said distractedly.

Noah gently cupped her face in his hands and ran the pads of his thumbs over her cheeks. Slowly, he studied her eyes. A smile lifted one corner of his mouth. "Having a woman respond to his marriage proposal with tears doesn't do much for a man's ego," he responded honestly.

Under the circumstances, she didn't want his simple admonition to get to her. But it did. And try as she might to fight it, she felt sorry for hurting his feelings.

"I'm not crying because you proposed to me…" She met his gaze and forgot what she was about to say.

She stirred uneasily as a warning flashed in her head. If she thought her car would make it through the snow, Dara would leave right now, because she wanted nothing more than to hole up in her room and hide under the covers, at least until the snow stopped falling. But she wasn't going anywhere, and she knew it.

"I wish I could tell you what you want to hear, Dara," he was saying. "I like you…like everything about you, but…"

He thinks you want to hear him say he loves you before— Why else was he looking at her with that expression on his face? What else could explain the way he'd softened his tone and tilted his head? He feels sorry for you!

She replayed the evening in her mind at fast-forward speed, scanning her memory for the thing she'd done or said that might have given him such a ludicrous notion. Love, she wanted to say, is the furthest thing from my mind at the moment.

But she hadn't spent all those years under the same roof with Gloria Mackenzie for nothing. Dara was a guest in Noah's house—a fact that wouldn't, *couldn't* change until morning at the earliest, thanks to the two-foot blanket of snow on the ground. She couldn't very well tell her host that he was beginning to sound like a conceited, self-absorbed man....

Or could she?

Dara opened her mouth, fully prepared to tell him what she thought of him *and* his buy-a-wife deal, when he slid an arm around her waist and led her to the couch.

"I owe you an explanation. Please sit down and let—"

"You don't owe me anything, least of all an explanation," she said, enunciating every word.

"Just humor me, then."

She sat, stiff and straight and silent, and listened.

"Francine...she was my wife—" He stopped and looked down, then started again. "It was cancer that took..." Noah inhaled sharply. "That..." He blew a stream of air through his lips before continuing. "I, ah, I don't make a practice of talking about this."

Suddenly, Dara felt sorry for him. "And you don't have to talk about it now," she said, her voice and manner softening.

"No, no. I need you to understand why I..."

Dara really didn't have any business listening to any of this. She barely knew the man, after all. If only she could go home, hide under her covers and go to sleep. At least then she wouldn't have to think about what Jake Mackenzie had done. Because if he hadn't stolen the money, Pinnacle wouldn't have hired a CPA firm to find it. So it was her father's fault, in a roundabout way, that Noah had gotten his absurd idea in the first place.

He stroked his mustache between thumb and forefinger. "I made a lot of promises to her at the end."

Well, at least while you're being Mother Confessor you won't have to think about Father Done You Wrong, she thought ruefully. "What kind of promises?"

"'Yes, honey, I'll remember your mother's birthday,' and 'No, honey, I won't forget the kids' piano lessons' and 'Of course I'll make sure they say their prayers' and…'" Facing forward, he leaned both elbows on his knees and clasped his hands in the space between, head down. His frown deepened, and so did his voice. "And I said I'd see to it they had a loving mother as soon as possible."

And loving him and her children as she had, Francine hadn't realized she was asking the impossible of him, Dara thought. Hadn't she seen how much he loved her, and that *because* he did, remarriage was the *last* thing on his mind? Dara sat quietly, watching, listening. Oh, he was trying hard, she could see, to hide his true feelings behind that stern expression and those no-nonsense words, but he was hurting. She knew because his voice took on a special softness, and a certain sadness-tinged-with-longing glinted in his eyes when he spoke of his wife.

Lord, Dara prayed, *will I ever know a love like that?* She tucked in one corner of her mouth. *Not likely, since there isn't a decent man left on the face of the earth.*

Now, that isn't fair, she quickly corrected herself. *Noah is decent enough. It's just that...*

Just that *what?*

"Look at me, Dara," he said, interrupting her reverie. He cupped her chin in a palm. "I've never told anyone any of this before. I wouldn't be telling you now, except..."

There was no mistaking the hitch in his voice. It made her wonder if she had the stuff it took to listen to him anymore. He was facing her now, but his gaze seemed to settle on everything in the room except her eyes.

"I grew up in an orphanage, raised by Franciscan brothers."

"Is that one of them," she asked, "in the picture on the mantel?"

He nodded. "That's Brother Constantine. Closest thing I ever had to a father."

"You looked like a good, sweet boy."

"By the time I was fourteen, you might say I was a 'hard case.'"

"Noah, really," she said gently, laying a hand on his forearm, "you don't have to tell me any of this. It's none of my business anywa—"

"Yes, I *do* have to tell you," he interrupted. "I made it your business when I asked you...when I..." He cleared his throat. "I was in trouble more than I was out of it. Cops and courtrooms were as familiar to me as my cot in the boys' barracks." He chuckled bitterly. "It got so bad for a while there that one particular judge knew me by my first name."

"I never would have guessed it," she admitted. "You seem so…so…like such a Goody Two-shoes."

He sat, silent and blinking for a second or two before a grin slanted his mustache. "You couldn't come up with something a little more macho than 'Goody Two-shoes'?"

She returned the smile. "Well, you *do* seem to be the type who goes by the book…a little uptight even."

"Uptight?" He laughed, but the merriment never quite made it to his eyes. "You make me sound like one of those bow-tie-wearing, pencil-necked nerds in flood pants and Ben Franklin glasses."

"Flood pants?"

"You know, with cuffs that end about three inches above your shoes?"

"I get it," she said.

In the privacy of her mind, she'd called him pompous. Arrogant. A single-minded, stubborn man who saw everything as black or white, period. She'd figured him for a self-righteous prig who judged all people by his own narrow belief system, and she hadn't needed any more proof of that than the way he'd pontificated about her father's crime. "Why would a man in his right mind do anything so foolish?" he'd asked that day in Jake's office.

A fussbudget, maybe. Supercilious, possibly. But she absolutely, positively, definitely did *not* see him as a nerd. "I never meant to imply you're stuffy and—"

"You think…you think I'm *stuffy?*"

"No. What I meant was—"

He held up a hand to silence her. "Too late to shut the barn door now. Bessie's out and chompin' oats."

"Hay."

"Huh?"

"Hay." She smiled slightly. "Horses eat oats. Cows eat grain or hay."

"Is that so?"

She nodded.

"I didn't know you were so well acquainted with farming."

"There's a lot you don't about me, Mr. Lucas."

"You promised to call me 'Noah,'" he reminded her. "And I know more about you than you realize."

At least their verbal frolicking had sidetracked them both—Dara from thoughts about her father, Noah from completing his confession. For a reason she couldn't explain, Dara didn't want to hear any more about his past, because she had a feeling it led directly to his talking about his love for his wife.

Because on the one hand, it was touching, the way he seemed to miss Francine as much today as the day he'd lost her; on the other hand, it sent a wave of jealousy coursing through her like none she'd experienced before. It made no sense, feeling this way about a man she'd just met. Besides, who was she to begrudge him his memories?

"I imagine life in a place like that could thicken anyone's hide," she said. She could almost picture him—young, impressionable, lonely...and angry, very angry.

"What happened to your parents?" she ventured.

Another shrug.

The gesture had been intended, she supposed, to convey that he didn't know. But she had a feeling he knew, and the pain of knowing caused a muscle to bulge in his jaw, made him clamp his hands together so tightly his knuckles turned white.

"How long did you live at St. Vincent's?"

"They tell me I was two when…" He shook his head. "And they boot you out of a place like that when you're eighteen—"

"But that's so young! How did you support yourself? Where did you live?"

"As I was about to say, they boot you out at eighteen unless you're a student."

She sighed with relief. "So you stayed?"

"Much as I hated the lack of privacy, the noise, never having anything to call your own, it was the only home I'd ever known. So I enrolled at Loyola—thanks to some not-so-subtle string pulling by Brother Constantine—signed up for a bunch of nonsense courses—art history, English lit, home economics." Another bitter chuckle. "Nothing that would take me anywhere near what I wanted to do with my life, but at least I had a place to call home, till they got wise to my scheme."

He may have had complaints about the place, but he'd loved it. "And what did you want to do with your life?"

He smiled a bit at that. "I wanted to teach. Math, to be exact. So kids like me wouldn't be afraid of numbers."

"Kids like you?"

No response.

"So why didn't you?"

"Teach, you mean?"

Dara nodded.

Another shrug. "Because I met Francine."

Her brows rose in confusion.

"I knew it'd take more than a teacher's salary to keep her happy. She'd been born with the proverbial silver spoon in her mouth, and I wasn't about to risk her father objecting to our relationship simply because I hadn't chosen a career with much earning potential."

"She loved you. What difference could your potential income have made?"

Noah laughed again, genuinely this time. "How old are you?"

"Thirty. What does that have to do with—"

"I'd think that by now, you'd have outgrown your naïveté." He winked, grinned. "It's kinda cute, though, the way you still have a kids'-eye view of the world."

"The way I still..." Dara clamped her teeth together. "How did you end up with a successful business of your own? And a CPA firm, of all things?" she asked, steering the conversation back on course.

"God seems to have blessed me with a talent for numbers. I have a good memory for them, and I know how to make them multiply."

"Stock market?"

"That, and other investments," he said, nodding. "I got a job my sophomore year as an intern with a CPA firm in New York—"

"I didn't know you were from New York."

"Syracuse, to be exact. Wormed my way into the Big Apple to further my education. That's where I met her—Francine, I mean. I had just graduated. Went to a fund-raising dinner for my boss. He was running for state senate, and her dad was a big contributor to the campaign...."

"You must have hit it off, that night at the fund-raiser."

"You could say that. Before I knew it, we were an 'item.'" He drew quotation marks in the air around the word. "I started saving every penny, almost from that first night, so I could one day open my own office. I wanted to take care of her in the manner to which she'd grown accustomed, to coin a phrase. She gave me a year to prove myself.'' He gave a proud nod of his head. ''I did it, too.''

Dara chose to ignore that last comment. If she hadn't learned anything else in life, she'd learned 'never speak ill of the dead.' ''Must have paid off, all that scrimping and saving. I mean, look at you now.''

''Yeah,'' he said, gaze traveling the room. ''Look at me.''

He didn't seem pleased with his material possessions. Not in the least bit. ''She must have been very proud of how hard you worked to gain her father's approval.''

''I guess.''

''You *guess?*''

''She used to say I pinched pennies so hard I made Lincoln cry.''

But you were doing it for her, Dara told him mentally. ''How'd you manage to save enough to open your own business in just a year?''

''I got a promotion at the firm. I was making good money, not spending a cent of it. When the weather was good, I worked for a landscaper, when it wasn't, I hired on as a painter. Didn't own a car—took the bus, instead—and lived in a one-room walk-up above an old woman's house. Cooked all my meals on a one-burner hot plate I bought at a flea market. Once a week, I'd splurge on dinner and a movie for Francine and me. Other than that, I made only deposits at the bank.''

''Must have made her feel like a queen to have someone working that hard to win her heart!'' she said, grinning.

"I don't know about that. But I loved *her* like crazy. Asked her to marry me the minute I hung out my shingle."

"And she said yes."

"Reluctantly."

"But...I thought—"

"She said she couldn't live in an apartment or a town house. Too much noise. Plus it wasn't a decent atmosphere to bring up kids, she said." He scrubbed a hand over his face.

"Noah, why are you putting yourself through this with a total stranger? I'm sure you have friends, lots of them, who'd be willing to—"

Elbows still balanced on knees, he slowly turned his head until their eyes met. "Something you ought to know about me, Dara...I choose my friends carefully. Very carefully."

But we're not friends, she thought. We haven't known each other long enough to—

"I know we've spent only a few hours together, but I know what I know."

A numbers man to the last, she thought.

"If you think I haven't given this marriage deal much thought, you're wrong."

"This 'marriage deal'?"

He continued as if he hadn't heard her. "For starters, I know you have a heart as big as your head, which in my opinion is why you're so terrific with kids. You can really empathize with them, see things from their point of view—a talent most of us soon leave behind.

"You're a hard worker, too, and I'll bet you say things like 'If you're going to do a job, do your best or don't bother.'"

Her father had drummed that very line into her head

more times than she could count. Did you put your life motto to the test when you were stealing the company's money, Dad?

"You're as honest as the day is long," Noah continued, "which is why this whole embezzlement situation surrounding your dad has your emotions in such a tangle."

This embezzlement situation, she thought, has more than my emotions in a tangle. Her heart, her head, her very soul had been affected by the news.

"You obey the speed limit, most of the time anyway, and you never cheat on your taxes. You have a little money squirreled away for the proverbial rainy day, and it doesn't take much to make you happy. Three square meals and a cot and you're content. Am I warm?"

He was right on target. But she was too busy reacting to the fact that she'd never heard anyone but Jake Mackenzie use that phrase to admit it. Two of her father's platitudes in less than a minute. Birds of a feather? she wondered, citing yet another cliché.

"You're sensitive, *very* sensitive, which is usually a good thing."

"When *isn't* it a good thing?"

"When you put others first and they don't seem to give a hoot about what you need. It makes you mad, if you're honest with yourself, real mad. Not because they're thoughtless...because..." He scooted closer, took her right hand in his left and said with soothing compassion, "It makes you mad because you don't like that *their* thoughtlessness hurts *your* feelings. You see it as a fault."

"Well, it *is*."

There was a tremor in his husky voice, as though

something had touched him deeply. "I haven't disagreed with anything you've said so far, but I draw the line at that one. From what I've seen, you don't *have* any flaws. I could put ads in every newspaper in the country and not find a person better suited to raise kids. *My* kids." He gave her hand a gentle squeeze. "You're a bargain, even at two hundred thousand—"

Dara snatched her hand away and stood abruptly. "I am *not* for sale, Noah Lucas! Not at *any* price!"

He blanched. "Of course you aren't. I—I didn't mean... I never meant to imply—"

"My father's reputation is important to me, very important. You're one hundred percent right about that. But I won't marry you just to preserve it. When I marry—*if* I marry—*love* will be the motivator, not money." She stalked over to the French doors, crossed both arms over her chest and stared out at the relentless snowfall. *Lord,* she prayed, *make it stop. The snow, the proposal, these* feelings...*make it all stop!*

She heard Noah leave the room. Had she made him angry? Hurt his feelings? Embarrassed him? Well, his offer to pay her to be his wife had made *her* mad, had downright *humiliated* her, and she didn't see him feeling all guilty about *that!*

Still, compared with Noah, she'd lived a life of comfort and ease from the day she was born. Dara didn't relish the idea that her "poor little me" attitude had added to his suffering, even a little. She felt the prickle of tears behind her eyelids, felt a sob gnawing in her throat. Guilt? she wondered. Or self-pity? Whichever, she could not give in to it. Not here. Not now. Dara clenched her jaw, girding herself with resolve. She would not cry. She *would not* cry!

She turned when Noah came into the room, arms

overflowing with pillows, blankets, sheets. He dumped his load onto the couch, shoved the coffee table out of the way. "It's a queen sleeper," he said, tossing a cushion aside. "I've never slept on it, but the salesman said—"

"No need to go to all that trouble," she said. "I'll sleep on it just as it is."

Nodding, he put the cushion back into place. "Okay. If you think you'll be comfortable," he said, his mellow baritone edged with control.

"I'll be fine, really."

"You know," he said, pocketing his hands and staring at the couch, "I never gave it a thought before tonight. Most folks would have turned their extra bedroom into a guest room, but I made a home office out of mine so I could bring work home, spend more time around the kids, you know?" He sighed with exasperation, smiled sheepishly. "I wish I could offer more comfortable accommodations, something with more privacy, but—"

"Noah, this is a beautiful room, what with the fire in the woodstove and everything. And the powder room is right across the hall. It'll practically be like having my own suite—once you go upstairs." She tried to smile. "It's my fault, after all, that I'm not sleeping in my bed tonight. If I had checked the weather from time to time, I wouldn't be stuck here, would I?"

He regarded her silently for a long moment before saying, "I left something out earlier."

Her raised eyebrows asked, "What?"

"A man wouldn't guess it to look at you, tiny as you are and all, but you're a tough little thing. And a natural-born nurturer, too."

"I rather like being seen as a 'tough little thing,'"

she said, laughing softly, "but nurturer? I don't think so."

"Well, *I* think so. Just look at you, chin up and shoulders back, stranded in a virtual stranger's house, and you're worried about *me*."

In truth, she *had* wanted to make him feel better. Had he seen it on her face? In her stance? It's positively spooky the way he knows these things about you, she told herself. "I'm not worried about you. Why would I be worried about you?"

"Because somehow, you know I feel like a complete jerk for making you think I wanted to *buy* you. And even though you were the one whose feelings got hurt, you're trying to make me feel like *less* of a jerk…though I don't deserve it."

Except for the "deserve it" part, Dara could only shake her head and sigh, because yet again, he'd hit the target.

Noah stood and walked toward her. He was beside her in an instant, hands on her shoulders, face mere inches from hers. "I'm sorry that I insulted you. Believe me, that's the last thing I wanted to do. I know it made me seem like a clumsy oaf, spelling out my plan the way—"

"Seem?" she put in, grinning.

"Okay. So I *am* a clumsy oaf." He returned her grin. "But I honestly thought it was a good idea, one that would help us both out of a bind." He spoke slowly, tentatively, as if testing her reaction.

Biting her lip, she looked away.

"It's getting late, and I know you're tired. I'll go now, so you can get some sleep."

But she was only half listening as she struggled with her thoughts. The way he looked just now, all apologetic and embarrassed, she'd almost agreed: it is a good idea.

"Want me to help you make up the couch?"

"No." She shook her head. "No, I'll be fine. I think I'll make myself another cup of tea, watch some television—if it won't disturb you, that is."

"Are you kidding? You could probably set off a bomb in here and we wouldn't hear it upstairs."

Dara nodded. "Good. Thanks. I'll see you in the morning."

He nodded, too. "Right. In the morning, then."

Without the slightest warning, his arms encircled her, one hand on the small of her back, the other cupping her nape. He stood for a long, silent moment, studying her with eyes that glittered like blue diamonds, lips pulled back in the barest hint of a smile. Stepping forward, he clasped her to him. She felt his soft breaths on her cheek, heard the quiet sigh issue up from deep inside him, felt the steady *thump, thump, thump* of his heart. The warmth of it was so complete, so sure, that Dara relaxed, resting her cheek against his chest. The embrace was almost unbearable in its tenderness, and she had no desire for it to end, ever.

But it must end. Now. Without looking away, she backed out of his grasp.

"Good night, Dara." He sighed. "Sweet dreams."

And he was gone.

She had a feeling she wasn't going to get a wink of sleep. Not because of the narrow couch. Not because of the snow that continued to fall. Not even because she had proof positive of her father's wrongdoing.

But because she'd be thinking of Noah Lucas, and the way his blue, blue eyes had lit up when she'd almost admitted his idea had merit.

Chapter Five

 ❧

Noah lay on his back, hands clasped under his head, and stared at the ceiling. A brisk wind had kicked up, went prowling and howling through the yard like an angry, lone wolf. As the snowflakes steadily hissed and pecked at the windowpanes, Noah was reminded that he had a houseguest.

Would Dara be asleep by now, snug and warm under the green plaid quilt he'd brought her? Had she put on the pajamas he'd tucked between the comforter and the sheets...the two-sizes-too-small pajamas Francine had bought for him half a dozen Father's Days ago?

If he closed his eyes, he could almost see Dara, the maroon silk of his pjs looking lush against her creamy skin as she sat cuddled in front of the cozy fire, long, dusky lashes dusting her freckled cheeks as she sought a peaceful night's sleep on a stranger's sofa.

He hadn't seen freckles on a female since grade school. Dara's dotted the bridge of her nose as if they'd been sprinkled there by a guardian angel. He wouldn't have noticed them at all if he hadn't pulled her into a hug under the sixty-watt lightbulb in the kitchen fixture. At the time, his only thought had been how incredibly *lovely* she was. Now, he thought, the faint, almost undiscernible speckles gave her a girlish, innocent look that went perfectly with chin-length auburn curls that bounced and bobbed with every turn of her head.

She had a quick, natural smile that immediately put others at ease. And those eyes, as big and wide as a doe's, glimmered with mischief when Angie and Bobby had challenged her to a spirited guessing game, then later glowed warm with sympathy when he described his pathetic past.

He'd told her he believed she was an honest woman, a hard worker with a heart bigger than her head. Well, she's all that and then some. The proof? Dara's attitude toward his blithe compliments. He'd clearly embarrassed her, as evidenced by her downcast eyes and the pink blush that had colored her cheeks. And that puzzled him. Puzzled him plenty. Because it had been his experience that most women lived to be flattered, whether the praise was bona fide or blarney. Surely a woman as gorgeous as Dara had had those attributes pointed out to her many times.

But if that was true, why hadn't she reacted the way other women he'd known before her had? "Oh, stop Noah," they'd say, giggling, striking shy poses, fluttering their lashes. "You'll make me blush."

Dara *had* blushed!

She's something else! he told himself, grinning into the darkness. There were likely a thousand clichés to describe her. Pretty as a picture. Sharp as a tack. Sweet as cotton candy. But there's nothing cliché about Dara! No, sir. She's one of a kind.

If he ever fell in love again, it would be with a woman like Dara Mackenzie.

He ran the thought past his brain another time or two. *If* he could fall in love again… Why can't you love again? he wondered.

But the answer was there, as plain as the night-black ceiling above him: he hadn't felt the heart-tugging stirrings of romance because he hadn't given it—or himself—a real chance.

Noah scrunched the pillow up under his neck, linked his fingers atop his chest. Have you been deliberately choosing women without a single solitary maternal bone in their bodies? Not deliberately, maybe, but subconsciously, he'd sabotaged the would-be relationships, right from square one.

Until now….

What was different about this one? Why was he being so ham-handed now?

Because didn't he owe it to her memory to try to keep the promise he'd made on the night Francine died?

You just answered your own question. Francine hadn't just asked him to "Get a woman in here, fast." She'd made her demand plain and simple: "They need a mother to look out for them. They need a woman's touch."

A woman's touch. Noah grunted, one side of his mouth tucked in, hands back up under his head again. Kids aren't the only ones who need a woman's touch.

Francine hadn't been the perfect wife, but she'd been pretty close. He'd never worn a shirt that hadn't been pressed to perfection. Never left the house with a button missing or unpolished shoes. She could have been a chef in some fancy restaurant if she'd wanted to, and the joke around the house was, her house was so clean folks could eat right off the floors. She'd alphabetized the spice rack, the pantry, the linens. And in the clothes closet, his shirts hung in color-coordinated order...grouped by sleeve length and fabric type.

Sometimes he thought she was too hard on the kids, insisting they tow the line, always, no matter what. But "mothering" was her job, and they were terrific kids. Who was he to argue with her methods, when the results were so obvious?

Besides, how many wives would insist that their husbands find their children a mother substitute, as soon as possible? And that's what this is all about, he reminded himself. Angie and Bobby.

From the moment of their conception, the children had given his life meaning and hope. Once born, it took little more than a toothless smile to brighten his dull world. And now that they were old enough to hold two-way conversations, they'd become companions of a sort, filling his lonely days with questions and observations that kept him from growing old before his time: "Why is the sky blue, Father?" and "God lives in the sky because He can see everything better from there." They were loving little beings that deserved to be loved right back...by a woman's gentle hands....

In the morning, he'd try again to convince Dara to marry him. He hadn't spent all those hours on his knees for nothing in the years since he'd lost Francine. Dara was the woman God intended him to spend the rest of his days with; Noah knew it as he knew the earth would continue spinning.

He'd phrase the question a bit more romantically this time, so she wouldn't be insulted, wouldn't feel like a heifer on the auction block. You're a buffoon, he chided, remembering the way he'd presented the idea initially, a callous dolt to have put it so bluntly. Francine would surely have scolded him soundly for being an insensitive lout. And the reason she'd chasten him would be simple: she wanted only the finest for her children, and how was he to provide the mother they needed if he scared the woman off?

Now there's an idea, he thought, sitting up. How would Francine have said the same thing?

As he gave it some thought, her voice echoed in his head. "The children need a good woman in their lives," she'd have insisted.

Yes, his kids deserved the best, and he'd done everything humanly possible to provide it. But he didn't know how to embellish an outfit for Angie, as Francine would have. And even he could see that the rooms of this new house were stark, almost puritanical in their plainness. But what was he to do? Even if he knew which doodads to buy, where would he put them!

A woman would know. And Dara, his prayers had convinced him, was that woman. Somehow, he had to convince her of that, for the children's sake. And for my sake, he added.

He'd be a good husband, as good as he'd been for Francine—maybe even better, thanks to her constant tutelage—but he'd never let himself forget who'd made it possible for those precious treasures named Angie and Bobby to come to live in his world.

Not even if Dara did agree to marry him.

Not even if one day he grew to love her.

Dara tossed and turned on the couch, wishing she'd let Noah open up the sofa bed. But even if he had, it wasn't likely she'd get any sleep.

Thoughts of him filled her mind as steadily as the snowflakes piling up against the French doors. Noah had said they had a lot in common. One thing they shared was a desire to say things straight out.

"It'll be a win-win situation," he'd said.

And maybe it would…if not for the fact that she had a little pride. Of course she wanted to clear her father's name, but that was no reason to get married…not even to someone as appealing as Noah Lucas. In the old days, plenty of people consented to arranged marriages to merge kingdoms, to pay debts, to secure a safe financial future for their families. But these aren't the old days! We're living in a modern world, where men and women marry for love! she told herself.

She rolled onto her back and focused on the ceiling fan above her head. Its brass trim reflected the bright-orange firelight glowing in the woodstove. But nothing, it seemed—not the soothing warmth of the fire, not the comforting heft of the downy quilt—could distract her from one dismal thought: This may well be your only chance at marriage and family, Dara Mackenzie.

She'd dated dozens of men since her sixteenth birthday but had rarely seen any of them on more than one occasion. "You're too picky, Dara," her mother would say when she dismissed yet another eligible bachelor. "Do you want to end up an old maid? Don't you want me to be a grandmother?"

Fact was, she wanted that more than just about anything. But if it meant she had to settle, then maybe she'd have to resign herself to life as a single woman.

"What's wrong with Jeremy?" her mother had wanted to know. "He's handsome and successful and—"

"And he talks too loud," Dara had said.

"What about Matthew?" she'd asked. "He owns his own business."

"And that's the *only* thing he can talk about."

"David seems nice...."

"But he isn't a Christian."

"I give up!" her mother had said, throwing her hands into the air in vexation.

But she hadn't given up. Instead, Gloria Mackenzie had scouted around town, searching out potential son-in-law material. Feeling she owed it to her mother to at least try to find a common interest with the men, Dara agreed to dinner at Tersequel's, movies at Palace Nine, sailing on the Chesapeake Bay. When she came home from the outings, the message light on her answering machine would be blinking. "Well," her mother's excited voice would ask. "How'd it go? Call me!"

It would have been nice seeing her mother bounce a grandchild on her knee before she died. Sometimes, great waves of guilt washed over Dara, knowing her "pickiness" had been the reason it hadn't happened.

She'd known what kind of man she wanted since her stuffed animal and dolly tea party days: a man exactly like her father.

But what kind of man stole nearly a quarter million dollars, for... Only the Lord knows why...so only the Lord should condemn him, she thought.

Since learning about his crime, Dara had tried to focus on his good qualities, such as the way he volunteered to play Santa at Johns Hopkins Children's Oncology every Christmas, stuffing his big green bag with toys he'd bought with his own money.

Now she had to wonder, had it been his money? And what about the summer when their next-door neighbor had been laid up with a back injury and he'd mowed the Jensens' lawn, from spring thaw straight to the first frost.

He'd gone grocery shopping once, all by himself, to buy food for a family displaced by a house fire. Had he paid the bill with money he'd earned? Or had he borrowed from Pinnacle's till to finance his charity work?

She hadn't been too nonplussed about her solitary status, because in her heart, Dara believed the Lord had chosen her mate long before she drew her first breath. It was merely a matter of finding him, she kept telling herself.

He'd be tall and handsome.

She guessed Noah to be five foot eleven, at least. And he certainly filled the "good-looking" category.

Her intended would be a good and decent man. One who was successful and hardworking. And he most certainly would be a devout Christian.

Like Noah Lucas....

The only negative, really, was the fact that she didn't love him and he didn't love her.

Dara sighed, rolled onto her side. Could you love him? she asked herself. Yes, she probably could—if she'd let herself—because he had all the qualities of a fine, upstanding husband and then some. His easy manner with his children, though, was probably Noah's most redeeming trait, because it had been that that made Dara see him as something other than a pencil-pushing stuffed shirt. When he looked at them, it was as if the rest of the world and everything in it ceased to exist. His voice automatically gentled when he talked to them, and the big hands that could probably perform that "strong man rips phone book in half" trick combed tenderly through their hair.

Those same hands had touched her, too, testing the softness of her cheeks, bringing her close enough to kiss.

What would it have been like, she wondered, if Noah had kissed you? Would the golden mustache have tickled? Would those full lips have felt as soft as they looked?

Exhaling harshly, Dara rolled onto her back again, frowning at the night-blackened blades of the ceiling fan. Stop it, she scolded. Stop it right now. You have no business thinking such things about a man you barely know!

But that wasn't true. Wasn't true at all.

She *did* know him, not in ways measured by calendar pages but in her heart. It didn't make sense that she felt so secure, so protected, so comfortable in his presence…in his arms. Didn't make sense that she understood the reasons he was drawn to Francine back when he'd been a lonely orphan. (Was he still an orphan? How old did a man have to be to shed that title?) Didn't make sense that when his voice had gone all ragged with pent-up grief, she'd wanted to console him with big hugs and little kisses and reassuring words, the way a mother comforts her child when a nightmare has wakened him.

That *especially* didn't make sense, because the feelings bubbling inside her now were not in the slightest maternal.

Yes, she could love him.

If she was honest with herself, she'd have to admit that maybe, just maybe, she loved him a little bit already.

* * *

The soft sounds of their pajama feet scraped across the kitchen's white-tiled floor, announcing their approach. Dara had been up for hours. Actually, she'd never gone to sleep at all. She sat at the table, sipping coffee and reading yesterday's newspaper, when Angie and Bobby ambled into the room, rubbing sleep-puffy eyes.

"What are you doing here?" Bobby asked around a yawn.

"The snow got too deep for me to drive home, so your dad invited me to sleep on your couch." They looked so adorable, so angelic with their tousled hair and sleep-pinked cheeks, that she wanted to hug them. "C'mere," she said, giving in to the feeling, "and gimme a hug." Dara extended her arms, and the children fell into them as if they'd been doing it every morning of their lives.

They smelled so sweet, like a beautiful blend of baby powder and sunshine, that she couldn't help but give each little forehead a lingering kiss. "Did you sleep well?"

Angie stepped out of the hug and, nodding, said, "I had a dream."

"Good or bad?" Dara asked.

"Very good." Smiling, the girl wiggled her dark eyebrows. "You married Father and became our new mother."

Heart pounding, Dara resisted the urge to gasp.

"That wasn't a good dream," Bobby said into Dara's sweater. She looked into eyes as blue as cornflowers. "It was a *great* dream!" Grinning, he tightened his hold on Dara. His cherubic smile broadened as he added, "You'd be a good mother, I think."

It was amazing how uplifting his words had been. "Why is that?"

"Because you're fun and nice and you give good hugs. And," he tacked on as mischief danced in his eyes, "you're very pretty, too."

She felt her spirit soar. "Well, thank you," she said simply. "Now, are you hungry?"

Both children nodded. "Father keeps the cereal in the pantry."

Opening the double doors, Dara inspected the shelves, where cold cereals of every brand and variety filled one whole shelf. "Say...there's pancake mix in here," she said over her shoulder. "How about a nice, tall stack of flapjacks, instead of cereal?"

"Flapjacks?" Bobby echoed, giggling. "That's a funny word." He marched around the kitchen, arms pumping, knees churning, repeating it like a chant. "Flapjacks, flapjacks, flapjacks."

"Be still, Bobby," Angie said. And to Dara, "He's such a baby."

He stopped midstep. Hands on his hips, he leaned forward. "I am *not* a baby!"

"No. You're six years old," his sister noted. "So act it."

The boy met Dara's gaze. Pouting, he asked, "Is marching for babies?"

Down on one knee, she pressed a palm to his cheek. "Have you ever been to a parade?"

"Of course we have," Angie volunteered in his stead. "Every Fourth of July."

Ignoring the girl's too-old demeanor, Dara said, "Then I'm sure you've seen all sorts of people—grown-ups included—marching. Musicians and soldiers and—"

"And *clowns!*" Bobby squealed.

"It's rude to interrupt," Angie said.

Dara made up her mind then and there to find out what was at the root of Angie's rigid, unchildlike behavior. For now, though, it seemed in everybody's best interests to distract her.

"Where do you guys keep the maple syrup?"

"'Guys' is not the proper way to refer to—"

"Angie," Dara said, hands on the child's shoulders, "how would you like to help me make pancakes?"

"Flapjacks!" Bobby corrected.

Dara grinned at him. "Flapjacks."

The girl's dark eyes brightened, widened, and a big smile lit up her face. "You mean it?"

"Sure!"

Angie clapped her hands and jumped up and down. "The only time we've ever had pancakes was in a restaurant. Father always burns them, and Mother never liked them." She turned to her brother, still bouncing like a rubber ball. "Pancakes! Right here in our own kitchen!"

"First," Dara instructed, "we'll need a great big bowl and one of those giant mixing spoons."

Bobby rummaged in a low cabinet, withdrew a stainless-steel bowl large enough for him to sit in. When he held it out in front of him, he all but disappeared behind it. "How's this?" he asked, his voice echoing in the cavernous space.

It was, in fact, five times larger than necessary, but Dara didn't have the heart to tell him that. "Perfect!" she said, putting it on the counter. "Now, how about a step stool?"

"In the pantry," Angie announced, dragging it from where it stood between the ironing board and a dust mop. The broom handle teetered for a moment before toppling from the pantry. "Watch out, Bobby!"

But her warning came a tick in time too late. The handle landed square on the back of the boy's head with a horrible *thump* that put him onto his hind end.

Dara didn't quite know what to make of the fact that the broom handle's blow had knocked Bobby off his feet. It wasn't as if it had been wielded, like a bat. Its slow descent surely would have smarted, but this? On her knees, she wrapped him in a fierce hug, kissing his temples and cheeks. "Oh, sweetie," she crooned, "are you all right?"

He was trying hard not to cry. "Yes, ma'am," he said around a sob. Wincing, he rubbed his head. "I'm fine."

"Well, then, what do you say we get busy on those pancakes."

He grinned past his tears. "Flapjacks," he corrected again.

Laughing, Dara helped him up. "Maybe we can have the *flapjacks* ready before your dad wakes up."

"He's sure gonna be surprised," Bobby said, rubbing the back of his head.

Dara couldn't help but notice the way he staggered those first few steps. *Lord*, she prayed, frowning slightly, *what's going on here?*

No sooner had she completed the thought than the boy was back to hopping and skipping around the kitchen. *Thank You!* she told God. And sighing with relief, Dara gathered the ingredients to make the main course.

After positioning the stool near the counter, she found a package of link sausage in the fridge, a dozen eggs and a loaf of unsliced Italian bread. Quickly and efficiently, she dumped the meat into a cast-iron skillet, and while it sizzled, she sliced the bread. "Have you ever made toast, Bobby?"

"No, ma'am."

But it was obvious by the excitement gleaming in his blue eyes that he'd love an opportunity to try. "Well, you're in charge of toast." She pulled open several drawers until she found the one where Noah kept the silverware. Handing the boy a butter knife and a stick of margarine, she slid two pieces of bread into the toaster and patted the stool. "Now, you have to be very, very careful not to touch anything until I tell you it's safe," she said as Bobby climbed onto the seat. "We don't want you to burn your fingers, now do we?"

Grinning from ear to ear, he said, "No, ma'am."

She tucked in one corner of her mouth. "Bobby, sweetie, would you do me a really big favor?"

He nodded. "Yes, ma'am."

Dara rested a hand on his shoulder. "Please don't call me 'ma'am.'" She wrinkled her nose. "Makes me feel like an old fuddy-duddy."

His brow crinkled. "What's a fuddy-duddy?"

Laughing, Dara drew him into a hug. "A fuddy-duddy is a stuffy crone."

"Oh," he said gravely, his expression and tone telling Dara he didn't know what a crone was, either. "What *would* you like me to call you?"

If it were up to her alone, they'd call her "Dara." Period. But since Noah never corrected them when they referred to him as "Father," like youngsters out of an old Dickens tale, she presumed he wouldn't approve of that. "How about calling me 'Miss Dara,'" she suggested. "You'll have to call me 'Miss Mackenzie' when we're in Sunday-school class, of course, so the other children won't be jealous, but when it's just us—''

"Why would they be jealous?" Angie wanted to know.

Standing, Dara slipped an arm around the girl's shoulders. "They might think that since we're, ah, special friends, I might give you special treatment."

"I get it," Bobby blurted. "They'll think we're teacher's pets!"

"Exactly!" Dara said. "Now, we'd better get busy, or your dad will be down before we even get started."

"I can't believe he's sleeping so late," Angie admitted. "He's usually the first one up. Most days, when we come downstairs, he already has our cereal in a bowl and our milk and juice poured."

Bobby nodded in agreement. "And a spoon on our napkin, with a vitamin next to the spoon."

Her heart skipped a beat as she acknowledged all the little, caring things he'd been doing since the children's mother died. She opened the cupboard where Noah kept the plates, took four from the shelf and carried them to the table. "Let's get this out of the way so we won't have anything to distract us."

In minutes, it seemed, breakfast was ready.

Noah came into the room as if on cue, his eyes still sleep puffy, sheet wrinkles dimpling his cheeks. He'd put on jeans—black ones this time—and a gray-and-white flannel shirt and, in place of the sneakers, a pair of well-worn leather loafers.

"How's a guy supposed to sleep with all these wonderful scents flittin' through the air?" he croaked.

Dara began filling their plates as Bobby giggled. "You sound like a frog, Father."

Grinning, Noah picked up his son, planted a noisy kiss on his cheek. "Sorry," he said, and proceeded to clear his throat.

"Now you sound like a bear," Angie put in.

He scooped her up, too, and pressed a kiss to her temple. "G'mornin', darlin'. Did you sleep tight?"

She nodded. And smiling, Angie said, "*You* sure slept late today. What happened? Did your alarm clock break?"

Gently, he put the children on the floor. "No," he said, focusing on Dara, "I just forgot to set it." And grinning, he added, "Don't know where my mind's been lately."

She'd already filled the juice glasses and now poured coffee into his mug. "Everything's ready," she announced. "Let's sit down before it gets cold. Angie and Bobby worked very hard to make you this feast."

Eyes widening, he smiled at his kids. "*You* made breakfast?"

"Yup," Bobby proclaimed.

"Well," Angie said hesitantly, "we helped."

"I couldn't have done it without them," Dara put in as Noah took his place at the head of the table and the children sat to his right and left, leaving the chair straight across from him for Dara, just like last night. She slid onto the caned chair seat and flapped a napkin across her knees. "Pass the salt, please?"

Grinning, Noah handed Bobby the butter dish, and snickering, the boy passed it down to Dara. She took it and, tucking in one corner of her mouth, said, "Thank you. May I have the salt shaker?"

This time Noah sent the pepper by way of Angie, whose mischievous grin made it apparent that Dara had been included in some sort of family game. She put the pepper shaker beside the butter dish and took a deep breath. "Thank you, Angie." And eyes on the girl's father, she tried again. "May I please have the salt?"

Smiling wider than ever, Noah put the plate of toast into his son's hands. And a moment later, the sausage platter, the pancake plate, even the jelly jar, sat in a tight cluster around Dara's place mat...everything *except* the salt.

Noah raised his left brow, looked at Angie, then Bobby. "She doesn't *seem* like the type who'd hog all the food," he said, feigning disgust, "but would you look at that?" He shook his head. "Didn't your mother teach you to share, Dara?"

Shoulders hunched, and hiding behind their hands, the children giggled.

"Funny. Very funny, you guys," Dara said, trying hard not to laugh herself. "And yes, my mother taught me to share." She stood, headed for Noah's end of the table. "She also taught me to take care of myself," she added, snatching the salt shaker. Calm as you please, she returned to her seat and sprinkled her eggs with the seasoning. "When I asked for the salt," she added, "I didn't think you'd as*sault* me with everything but!"

The Lucases laughed as she put the shaker down with a solid *thud*, and aiming a perfect Stan Laurel smile at Noah, Dara speared a slice of sausage. "Mmmm." She closed her eyes. "Dee-*lish*-us."

"So what do you think, kids?" Noah began. "Isn't Miss Mackenzie pretty first thing in the morning?"

"*I* think she's pretty *all* the time," Bobby admitted.

He tousled the boy's hair. "When you're right, son, you're right."

Dara felt the heat of a blush brightening her cheeks,

and wished for a legitimate excuse to leave the table, at least until the color faded. Unable to think of one, she tried a different tack. "After we get the breakfast dishes cleaned up, what say we go outside and build snow forts."

"Snowmen, you mean."

Dara gave Angie's hand a gentle squeeze. "No, sweetie. I mean snow forts. First we'll make big bricks, then stack them one on one. We'll build two walls and make a whole pile of snowballs and split up into teams, and—"

"I get it!" Bobby hollered. "We'll duck down behind the walls and throw the snowballs at one another!"

"You mean...like a pretend war?"

"Oh, no-o-o, Angie. Not a *pretend* war," Dara replied in a deliberately serious voice. "I play to win!"

"Then I want to be on your side!" Bobby yelled.

"No," Angie protested. "*I* want to be on her side!"

Laughing, Dara sat back in her chair. "Kids, kids," she said, waving her hands like white flags. "I don't think I've ever felt more wanted in my life, but there's enough of me to go around. Here's how we'll solve our little dilemma."

"What's a...a dalemon?" Bobby wanted to know.

"Not dalemon, silly." Angie sighed. "*Dih*-lemma. It means problem." With a smug smile, she looked at Noah. "Doesn't it, Father?"

He nodded, then focused on Dara again. "So what's the solution to our *dih*-lemma, Teach?"

"First, it'll be the boys against the girls, then Bobby and me versus you and Angie."

"Then the grown-ups against the kids!" Bobby started packing food into his cheeks like a chipmunk storing up nuts for a long, hard winter. "Hurry up!" he mumbled around a mouthful. "Let's finish breakfast so we can go outside!"

Frowning, Angie groaned. "He's behaving like a nasty little pig. Tell him not to talk with his mouth full, Father."

Her scolding didn't seem to have fazed Bobby. Grinning impishly, he stuffed even more food into his mouth. "Better make that 'piglet.'"

"Piglet?" Angie echoed, crossing both arms over her chest.

He swallowed, washed down his mouthful with a swig of orange juice. "Well, you said I was acting like a baby, now you say I'm acting like a pig. And a baby pig is called…" He lifted both shoulders and held out his hands, inviting his sister to finish the sentence for him. When she didn't, he climbed off his chair and carried his empty plate to the sink. "Thanks for the flapjacks, Miss Mac—I mean, Miss Dara." And slinging an arm over his father's shoulder, Bobby added, "Thanksgiving is next week, isn't it?"

Noah nodded. "I believe it is. Why do you ask?"

Bobby wrinkled his nose. "'Cause…I remember last Thanksgiving, that's why."

"And the one before that, and the one before that," Angie put in, "when you burned the turkey and the stuffing was all mushy and—"

Laughing good-naturedly, Noah held up a hand. "Yeah, yeah, I remember."

"So I was just wondering…" Bobby smiled at his Sunday-school teacher. "Can Miss Dara cook our Thanksgiving dinner?"

Silence blanketed the table as Noah's gaze met Dara's. "I think…I think that's a great idea," he started. "Providing she doesn't already have other plans."

You and your great ideas, Noah Lucas, she thought as they all stared, waiting to see if she'd accept or decline the invitation. As recently as yesterday morning, she'd wondered whether to eat her turkey dinner at the Westview Inn or pop a TV dinner into the microwave. Her grandparents had all joined the Lord decades ago, and since her parents had both been only children, Dara had no family to spend the holiday with. "I, ah, I'd love to."

"You'll have to make me a list," Noah said, standing, "things I'll need to pick up at the grocery store." And stacking plates, he added, "And we'll help, won't we, kids?"

Beaming, both children nodded.

"If it's all the same to you…"

It was as though someone had come along and wiped their smiles away with a vigorous washcloth. They think you've changed your mind, she realized. "If it's all the same to you, I'd rather do the shopping myself. Sometimes I have a memory like a noodle strainer, I don't want to take a chance on forgetting something on the list."

Three sighs of relief wafted around the room as Noah put the plates beside the sink. "It's all settled, then," he said, gathering silverware. "But you'll have to let me reimburse you for the food."

Two flapjacks, three sausages and an egg were left over. She put them on a clean plate. "I don't *have* to, Mr. Lucas."

"'Noah.'"

Her heartbeat doubled as she read the warmth in his eyes. She shot him the Stan Laurel grin again. "So where do you keep the plastic wrap, *Noah?*"

Chapter Six

"Everything was delicious," Noah said as together, they cleared the dishes. "And the table looked as though it was set to welcome the queen of England."

"I wonder why I always eat like there's no tomorrow on Thanksgiving," she asked, pretending she hadn't heard his compliments.

"Maybe because you eat like a bird the rest of the year? You couldn't weigh a hundred pounds soaking wet."

"One hundred fifteen," she admitted. "And for your information, certain species of birds consume as much as five times their own weight every single day."

"Horses and cows...and birds, too, eh?"

"Excuse me?"

"Horses eat oats, cows eat—"

"Oh. That." Dara shrugged, remembering the conversation they'd had the night she was snowed in. Sliding the leftover turkey onto a platter, she explained, "I read a lot. And watch cable TV."

"Watch a lot of cooking shows? That turkey looked picture-perfect."

Wrapping the leftovers in aluminum foil, Dara laughed. "The secret to that is an oven that heats evenly and some olive oil, brushed on the breast every half hour."

"Olive oil? Not butter?"

She shook her head.

"And what about that stuffing? I thought I tasted cloves in there."

She cocked an eyebrow. "You don't expect me to reveal *all* my kitchen tricks, do you?" A second ticked by. "And you're right. But just a pinch."

Noah smiled. "I was just about to say that a woman has a right to certain, ah, secrets." He was on his knees in front of the refrigerator, rearranging the contents to make room for the holiday leftovers. "Thanks for sharing. And by the way," he said over his shoulder, "I've been meaning to tell you since we sat down to eat…"

Dara braced herself for another meal-related compliment.

"You look gorgeous today."

She'd arrived at nine sharp, wearing sneakers and a pale gray sweatsuit. Noah and the kids helped her carry ten bags of groceries into the kitchen but hadn't noticed the small rucksack in her trunk. Once the bird was in the oven and the rest of the meal well under way, Dara had sneaked outside to grab it. Minutes later, in the powder room just off the kitchen, she washed up and unpacked a long, flowing skirt of deep red silk and a cream-colored shirt with puffy pirate sleeves.

"More like *gorged,*" she said, in an attempt to ignore the compliment.

As usual, she'd worn an assortment of southwestern-style jewelry: dangly earrings made of hammered brass, a black rope-style necklace carrying a wolf's head carved from jade, a sleeping wolf cub hanging from a silver bracelet. She'd dusted a thin layer of mossy green shadow on her eyelids, stroked a bit of brick red lipstick on her mouth and, bending at the waist, fluffed her chin-length curls. It had taken fifteen minutes to complete the ''look,'' but Dara hadn't expected him to comment on it.

''What color would you say your hair is?'' he asked, interrupting her reverie.

''My mother said auburn. I say brown with red highlights.''

''Reminds me of the chestnuts my mother-in-law always roasts at Christmastime.'' Standing, he shut the refrigerator door. ''And what about your eyes?''

''What about them?''

''What color are they? I mean, they're not brown or green, and they're sure not blue.''

''Hazel.''

''But...I always thought hazel was more golden, like a lion's eyes.''

She shook her head. ''Ever seen a hazel tree?''

''I'm not sure.''

''They're in the birch family, and their nuts—filberts to some—are a light reddish brown.'' She shrugged and smiled, as if to say, Hazel, get it? ''Chestnuts, hazelnuts...guess you'd have to say I'm as nutty as they come.''

He chuckled.

''*Father!*'' Angie's scream put an abrupt end to their friendly banter. ''*Father, come quick!*''

Dara knew in an instant that the cry had not been inspired by playful roughhousing. And Noah knew it, too, as evidenced by the fact that his playful expression had turned to stone. *"Father!"* Angie called again as Noah and Dara raced for the foyer. *"Fa-ther!"*

"Angie," Noah said, rounding the corner. "What is it?"

"B-B-Bobby," she sobbed, pointing at the floor. "He was r-r-running a-a-and he slipped on the r-r-rug."

Bobby lay, still and quiet, in a rumpled heap on the slate. Instinctively, they got onto their knees, Noah cradling his unconscious son in his arms, Dara trying to comfort his hysterical daughter.

She noticed it the instant he lifted Bobby's head from the floor...a tennis-ball-size pool of bright red blood. So as not to alarm Angie or Noah, she touched Noah's arm and with a nod indicated the spot.

Eyes widening when he saw it, Noah immediately inspected the back of Bobby's head. "We'd better get him to the hospital, get some X rays done. Could be a concussion or—"

"Should I call 911, Father?"

"No time for that." Noah reached out, squeezed her hand. "Be a good girl and bring me the big quilt off your brother's bed, will you?"

She was off and running before he could thank her, and the instant she was out of sight, he turned to Dara. "I hate to impose, after all you've already done for us today, but would you go with us to the hospital, hold him while I drive?"

"Of course," she said softly, squeezing his arm. "I'll get a cloth for his head."

Dara ran to a nearby bathroom, where she quickly wet a hand towel. After padding it up, she handed it to Noah, who applied it to the back of Bobby's head. Dara was relieved to hear the child softly moan, though he did not totally regain consciousness.

In the month since she'd met them, Dara had grown to love the Lucas children almost as much as if they were her own. They reminded her of little flowers, wilted after being left too long in the sun without water. Some tender loving care, a bit of her motherly attention, and they seemed to spring back to life, bright and beautiful as ever. She'd always been the kind of teacher who considered the kids in her classes hers, but these two were different, special, and they had been, right from the start.

Angie thundered down the stairs, dragging the comforter behind her. "Please don't run, sweetie," Dara said, holding out her arms. The girl spilled into them as Noah wrapped the thick quilt around his son.

They got to their feet simultaneously. Dara pulled Angie's coat from the hall tree, helped her into it, then draped Noah's leather bomber jacket over his shoulders. The last time she'd been here, Dara noticed that he kept his keys in a carved wooden bowl on the foyer table. Shrugging into her own coat, she grabbed them with one hand and yanked open the front door with the other.

Noah, cradling Bobby close, half ran onto the porch. The minute Angie was out the door, Dara followed, slamming the door behind her. She ran ahead, helped Angie into the back seat, then slid into the passenger seat. "Don't forget to buckle your seat belt, sweetie," Dara called over her shoulder as Noah gently deposited Bobby into her waiting arms.

Noah raced around to the driver's side, and froze, looking helpless and confused, worried and afraid, as he patted his pockets in search of the keys.

"Right here," Dara said, jangling them in the air.

He breathed a heartfelt "Thank God," and climbed into the car. "Thanks," he said, voice hoarse and tense as he made several unsuccessful jabs at the ignition.

She laid a comforting hand on his left arm. "Don't worry, Noah. It'll be all right," Dara whispered understandingly.

He took a deep breath and revved the motor. "I hope so."

They sped over back roads and boulevards en route to the hospital, emergency flashers blinking, headlights burning bright, horn honking. "Where's a cop when you need one?" Noah demanded of no one in particular.

"Should we pray for a police officer to stop us, Father?"

He glanced in the rearview mirror and smiled stiffly. "No, sweetie, that's all right. I'm just blowin' off a little steam is all. Don't pay any attention to me."

Hugging Bobby tighter, Dara pressed the hand towel against the gash in the back of his head. *Sweet Jesus,* she prayed, *be with us.*

"Our Father who art in heaven," she prayed aloud, "hallowed be Thy name."

"Thy kingdom come, Thy will be done," Angie joined in, "on earth as it is in heaven."

"Give us this day our daily bread," came Noah's ragged baritone, "and forgive us our trespasses..."

They prayed fervently, the three of them, all the way to Howard County General. And halfway through the second recitation, as if in answer to their prayer, the hospital's slant-roofed emergency entrance came into view.

"Praise God!" Noah shouted as he wheeled the car to a screeching halt near the red curb.

Dara didn't hesitate for an instant. She was out the door, Bobby's limp body pressed close, even before Noah could suggest that she head on in while he parked the car. "Stay with your dad, Angie," she said, shoving the door shut with the heel of her shoe. "I'll see you inside in just a minute."

She looked back in time to see the girl nod, her wide, frightened eyes brimming with tears. *Father in heaven,* Dara prayed as she rushed through the ER doors, *please watch over these little children.* As the double doors hissed shut behind her, she remembered Noah's worried, terrified face and quickly added, *Watch over their father, too.*

Three hours and four foam cups of vending machine coffee later, Noah found Dara and Angie huddled together in the dimly lit waiting room. "He has a concussion," he said, slumping into the chair beside his little girl. "The doc says it could be serious."

Angie climbed into his lap and buried her face in the crook of his neck. "Oh, Daddy," she sobbed, "it's my fault. It's all my fault!"

She hadn't called him Daddy since she was in diapers. Francine always said it sounded too middle class, too juvenile, and began insisting she call him "Father," instead. He'd hated it from the get-go, and the one time he said so, his wife had pitched such a fit that he'd decided the new title wasn't nearly as painful as the price he paid complaining about it. "Aw, Angie, honey," he said, heart throbbing with an odd mix of joy and relief at hearing the simple word, "it isn't your fault."

"B-but...but he tripped on the rug. It was my idea to run around and make him chase me."

Noah held her tighter, stroking her hair. His heart hammered with love and dread. "No, darlin'," he told her, "it was not your fault. It was just an accident. You mustn't blame yourself. Promise?"

His quiet words seemed to calm her slightly. Nodding, she took a dragging, shuddering breath. "Is he going to die, Father?"

Back to "Father" again already, are we? he thought with a pang of regret. "Of course n—"

"If he dies, he'll go to heaven, won't he? To be with Mother?" She seemed to shrink into the chair's nubby blue upholstery. Arms crossed tightly over her chest, she began to cry. "Well, I don't care! I—I don't *want* him goin' to Mother," she blubbered. "She has God and the angels to keep her company. She *always* got what she wanted. What's she want to go an' take Bobby away from us for?"

Under ordinary circumstances, Angie never would have ended a sentence in a preposition, let alone drop her *G*s and *D*s; Francine had drilled proper diction and grammar into the children's heads from word one.

But these were far from ordinary circumstances.

"Your mother didn't have anything to do with this." He grasped her hand, held it tight. "I can promise you that."

He turned to Dara, linked the fingers of his free hand with hers. "I wonder if you'd mind driving her home," he said. "No telling how long it's going to take them to finish all the tests." He glanced at Angie, focused on Dara once more. "I think being here is only scaring her."

Leaning forward, Dara whispered, "Of course I'll

drive her home, Noah, if that's what you want.'' She, too, glanced at the girl, who sat sniffling in the waiting room chair. ''But if I were her, I'd be a lot less scared if I could wait right here with my dad.''

He heaved a long, exhausted sigh. ''Maybe. Maybe you're right.'' Slipping an arm around Angie's slender shoulders, he pulled her as close as the chair arms would allow. ''You want Miss Mackenzie to take you home? You could get into your pjs, watch some TV...''

Her dark eyes widened with fear and unease. ''No! I want to stay until Bobby is all right again!''

He stroked her dark, satiny hair. ''Okay, okay. It's okay, baby. We'll all wait right here together, okay?''

''Okay,'' she blubbered.

To Dara, he said, ''Okay?''

Smiling gently, she nodded. ''Okay.''

Angie wiped the tears from her eyes, giggled a bit at their repetitious conversation. ''Is it okay if I go to the bathroom?''

''Okay,'' he said, winking.

Dara stood beside the girl. ''Is it okay if I come with you?''

''Okay,'' Angie said, grinning past her tears.

''Okay, you two,'' Noah said, ''get a move on.''

Dara met Noah's eyes and smiled. He smiled right back, calmed by the certainty that his little girl was in loving, gentle hands. His instincts about her had been right on target. *Dara is so good for the kids,* he thought, watching them head down the hall. As they disappeared into the ladies' room, he leaned forward, held his head in his hands.

She'd been so calm, so rational, in the great rush to get Bobby ready for the ER. Her reassuring voice had soothed Angie, had assuaged his own fears. Somehow, she'd had the presence of mind to grab their coats, to lock the door, to remind Angie to buckle up. And even as they'd sped over back roads and boulevards en route to the hospital, her rock-steady recitation of the Lord's Prayer had quietly reassured him.

When he'd walked into the emergency room, he could hear her, warning the nurses and doctors in attendance that they'd have to answer to *her* if Bobby's injury wasn't taken care of—*immediately.*

Had they gone to work straightaway because of her implied threat? Or would they have gotten right down to business anyway? Only God knows, he thought, smiling.

If she noticed the blood on her near-white blouse, she hadn't mentioned it. If she was aware Bobby had bled on her silk skirt, too, she gave no indication of it. Even Francine—once things calmed down—would have pitched a fit if something like that had happened to one of her best outfits.

There was no reason for Dara to be here, enduring these long, worrisome hours as he and Angie waited for news about Bobby's condition. Surely she had better things to do at home—lesson plans to write, papers to grade, people to see and all that. She'd shopped for, cooked and served the best Thanksgiving dinner he'd ever eaten, bar none. And then cleaned up willingly…and there had been no price to pay for allowing her to fuss over him like a mother hen. Dara wasn't like any woman he'd ever known.

Admit it, you big dumb cluck. She's good for you, too.

Angie and Dara had stayed with him in the waiting room until midnight. It was only because Dara promised to bring her back first thing in the morning that Angie willingly went home without a fuss, even then. It was a good feeling, knowing Dara had taken his car, tucked his sleepy little girl into the front seat and driven the four and a half miles to his house. Was an even better feeling knowing Dara would be with Angie all night long. *Wouldn't surprise me a bit if she got right into bed with Angie and crooned lullabies till she falls sleep,* he told himself, smiling.

"Mr. Lucas?"

The raspy voice interrupted his musing. Standing, Noah faced Collin Tilley, the neurologist who'd been on duty when they'd brought Bobby into the ER.

"I wonder if you'd mind coming with me for a minute?"

Noah followed the doctor from the curtained cubicle, down a wide hallway, into a small office.

"Can I get you anything?" Tilley asked. "Coffee? Soda?" He pulled open a desk drawer, revealing a stash of packaged cookies and candy bars. "Peanut butter crackers?"

"No. No, thanks," Noah said, grinning slightly as he waved the offer away. "How's my boy?"

The doctor flopped unceremoniously onto a creaking secretarial-type chair and gestured toward the only other seat in the room...a chrome-legged, black-padded stool. "Please, have a seat."

Noah sat, hung the heels of his hiking boots on the stool's bottom rung, waited...and prayed.

Tilley ripped into a chocolate bar. "Haven't had anything to eat since I got here," he said, taking a bite. "Sure I can't interest you in something?"

"No. Thanks."

"Bobby suffered a serious concussion when he hit

that slate floor.'' Tilley leaned forward, perched both elbows on the desktop. ''But tell me, has he ever hit his head before?''

Shrugging, Noah said, ''Sure. Especially when he was learning to walk.''

The doctor held up a hand. ''I mean *real* falls. Not necessarily something that would render him unconscious, but hard hits to the head.''

Noah gave it a moment's thought. ''No. Nothing like that. He fell out of a tree once, broke his arm.'' He shrugged helplessly. ''But, then, he's always been an eager-to-please kid. Maybe he *did* hurt himself somewhere along the line and didn't want to complain.'' Noah's frown deepened and he, too, leaned forward. ''Why?''

The doctor slid the X ray from its large manila envelope, held it up to the fluorescent light. ''See this?'' he asked, using his silver pen as a pointer.

Noah nodded at the faint gray line.

''I'd need an MRI to know for certain, but I'd guess it occurred one, maybe two, years ago.'' The ballpoint pen moved a hair to the right. ''This is the new damage.'' He followed the track of a slightly larger, longer fissure in Bobby's skull. ''This dark area around it is blood. And see the swelling here?'' Tilley gave Noah a moment to take in the information, then returned the X ray to its holder. ''Part of the problem,'' he said, sitting back, ''is that for some reason, the first injury never completely healed. When he fell this time, Bobby redamaged the same tissue.''

Heart pounding, Noah swallowed, squeezing one fist, then the other. *Lord in heaven*, he prayed, *it sounds like he's saying there's permanent brain damage.* ''He'll…he'll be all right, won't he?''

The doctor put down his candy bar and leaned forward. "Mr. Lucas, are you a religious man?"

"I fail to see what that has to do with—"

"May I suggest you pay a little visit to our chapel? It's on the lower level, right across from the—"

Noah got to his feet so quickly, the wheeled stool rolled across the floor and slammed into a filing cabinet. "Listen, Tilley," Noah thundered, "don't pull that hem-and-haw stuff with *me*. If my boy's in trouble, I need to hear it, *now*. Just give it to me in plain English," he demanded, taking his seat again.

Tilley, teeth clenched and hands folded tight on his desk, looked straight into Noah's eyes and launched into his diagnosis. "Fair enough," he began. "It's like this. Bobby's brain is swollen. There's some bleeding in there, too—not enough to endanger his life, but enough to put pressure on his optical nerves." He took a deep breath, rubbed his tired eyes. "You sure you want to hear this no holds barred?"

Noah clenched his teeth. "No holds barred."

Tilley sighed. "When your son wakes up, he may not be able to see."

"At all?"

"Right."

Every nerve was tingling, every muscle tensed. Noah thought he'd girded himself for bad news, that he'd been prepared to hear Tilley say that Bobby might lay unconscious for a day, maybe two. But *blind?* "How long?" he asked, not recognizing his own grating voice.

"Now, here's where science fails, and even the most pompous doc doesn't have an answer. I wish I could predict what'll happen, Mr. Lucas, but I can't. It depends on so many things—the swelling, mostly."

"So he could be…he could be—" Noah swallowed, hard, unable to make himself say the word.

"There's no reason to believe it'll be permanent."

"Well," he said, getting slowly to his feet, "I asked you to give it to me straight. Can't have it both ways, now can I?"

Tilley extended a hand. "No. I suppose not."

Noah shook the doctor's hand, then turned to leave. "Can I see him now?"

"Sure. Sure. We've got him on a glucose drip and oxygen, so don't be alarmed by the tubes and—"

"I lost my wife to leukemia a couple years back, Doc. I've seen every gizmo you can attach to a person."

"Sorry," Tilley said again. "Don't worry if he doesn't come to right away."

"How long will he be out?"

Shaking his head, Tilley said, "Hours? Days?" And shrugging helplessly, he held out his hands.

"Maybe that's a blessing in disguise," Noah said, opening the door.

Tilley picked up his candy bar. "Why's that?"

"'Cause I can use the time to figure out how I'm gonna explain to my six-year-old son why he can't see."

"One of the nurses let me use her cell phone," Noah said in a barely audible voice. "I don't want to leave him, not even for a minute. Because if he wakes up and can't see, he'll be scared out of his wits."

"Oh, Noah, I wish there were something I could do for you."

"For *me*?" A short, grating laugh escaped his lungs. "*I'm* not the one who might go blind," he growled.

"No," she said softly, sweetly, "but you still can't see."

"See what?"

"That you need to be gentle with yourself *and* with Bobby, because I have a feeling that if he does lose his sight, it'll be as hard on you as it'll be for him."

He'd been with the boy in the intensive care unit for nearly three hours now, listening to the steady blip of heart monitors, the heave-wheeze of respirators, the murmur of voices at the nurses' station, the occasional peal of a phone. The sound of her voice was like a healing salve on his heart. "I didn't mean to bark at you," he said.

"You have absolutely nothing to apologize for, Noah. If Bobby was mine, I don't know if I'd be holding body and soul together as well as you are."

In the semidarkened room, the window separating ICU from the hallway became a mirror of sorts. He caught a glimpse of himself, and sent a silent prayer of thanks heavenward that she couldn't see his trembling hands, his tousled hair, his rumpled clothes. He couldn't see the color of his eyes in the varying shades of gray that were his reflection, but Noah knew if he could, his eyes would be puffy and bloodshot. Keeping body and soul together? It made him chuckle. "Are you kidding? *You're* the most in-control person I've ever met."

"It's easy to be rational and reasonable when you're on the outside looking in."

Noah wanted to tell her she wasn't on the outside, at least not in *his* mind. That as far as he was concerned, Dara was part of the family, especially now. But Bobby moaned softly, distracting him. "I think he might be comin' out of it," he whispered excitedly into the phone. "The nurse said when he wakes up, they might be able to move him into a regular room."

"Go, then," she said. "See to Bobby. And don't you worry about anything here. Angie's sleeping like a baby, has been for hours."

He ran a hand through his hair, took a deep breath. "You're a godsend. I mean it. I don't know what I'd do without you right now."

"You'd do fine." She hesitated, a mere fraction of a second, then quoted him exactly: "'You're the most in-control person I've ever met!'"

He could hear the smile in her voice, and it inspired one of his own. "Thanks, Dara."

"You're welcome, Noah. Now, get off this phone and give that sweet boy of yours a hug and a kiss from me."

I could use a hug and a kiss myself right about now, he admitted silently. "I'll call you if anything changes."

"Call me even if it doesn't," she said. "And Noah?"

"Yeah?"

"I'll be praying for you both."

"Thanks," he said again, and hung up.

Angie padded into the kitchen at 6:00 a.m., lower lip jutted out in a worry-pout. "Can we go back to the hospital now?" she asked, tiny fists rubbing sleep from her eyes. "I want to see Bobby."

"Sure we can, sweetie. Soon as we get something warm and nourishing into your tummy." She managed to coax Angie to eat half a bowl of instant oatmeal and take a few sips of orange juice before they went back upstairs to get dressed.

Once they arrived at the hospital, Dara settled Angie in the waiting room. The nurses promised to keep an eye on the girl while she looked in on Noah. "*Some-body* has to talk some sense into him," one of them said. "He won't be any good to the kid if he wears himself out. He's been sitting there like that for four straight hours," she whispered, shaking her head. "I declare, I don't think he's left that boy's side long enough to get a cup of coffee or use the men's room!"

Dara peered through the window at Noah, slouched low in the chair, one arm flung over the side, the other bent at the elbow, palm shading his eyes. The way he half sat, half lay, long legs out in front of him, he appeared to be asleep.

But Dara knew better. He'd phoned her every half hour since she'd taken Angie home at midnight, and his voice had grown increasingly tense with each call. Remembering the exhausted, edgy sound of it had kept her pacing and praying—for Bobby *and* his daddy— all through the night.

Shoving open the door, Dara tiptoed inside. "Noah?" she whispered. "You awake?"

"Yeah," he grunted. "What're you doing here?"

She'd tucked Bobby's favorite stuffed dog under one arm, held a cup of coffee in one hand and a sandwich in the other. "Seeing to it you take care of yourself, that's what," she said matter-of-factly. "*You're* certainly not doing a very good job of it."

He tilted his head left and right to work the kinks out of his neck. "Thanks, but no, thanks. I'm not hungry."

"I don't care."

He cut her a frazzled frown before sitting up. Then,

planting both feet on the floor, he accepted the coffee, took a long, slow sip.

"Angie is in the waiting room, coloring with one of the nurses. She wants to see Bobby, so she can give him this." Dara held out the stuffed animal.

Noah rubbed his temples. "That's m'girl, always thinkin'." He glanced at Bobby and grimaced. "Did she sleep well?"

"I checked on her every fifteen minutes or so. She was out like a light every time I peeked in."

"Good, good." He nodded. "Did she give you any trouble about eating breakfast? Sometimes, she—"

"Unlike certain people who shall remain nameless," Dara began in her best teacher's voice, "Angie realizes that unless she keeps up her own strength, she won't be of any use to anyone." She held the sandwich out to him. "It's turkey. I brought it from home."

Both eyebrows rose on his forehead. "Home?"

She felt her cheeks redden. "I mean, I, ah, I brought it from your house."

Noah shot her a weary half grin, took hold of the sandwich and unwrapped it. "You were right the first time," he said, biting into it.

Dara walked around to the other side of Bobby's bed. "Has he come to yet?"

"No. Couple of times I thought he might, but no."

She leaned over, kissed his forehead. "Hey, sweet boy," she crooned, "how long are you planning to sleep?"

Almost immediately, his blond lashes fluttered.

Dara tucked the panda under his arm. "Angie thought Ming might be missing you."

Wincing as he moved his head from side to side, he

automatically hugged the dog tight. "Miss Dara?" he croaked out. "I have a headache."

"I'm not surprised," she whispered. *Dear God, let him see. Let him be able to see, Sweet Jesus!* she chanted mentally. "That was some fall you took." She gave him a little hug. "Oh, sweetie, I'm so glad you're awake!"

Vigorously rubbing his eyes, he whimpered, "Where…where's my father?"

"Here, son," Noah said, one hand gripping Bobby's, the other combing through the boy's hair. "I'm right here."

Knuckling his eyes now, Bobby breathed in short, raspy gasps. "Daddy? I can't…I—"

Noah slid an arm under the boy's neck. "I'm here, son."

Tears filled Bobby's alarm-widened eyes and he pressed the heels of his palms to his temples. "Daddy, why does it hurt so bad?"

"You hit your head when you fell, remember?"

Bobby turned toward Dara. She knew in an instant that he could see her, for his bright-blue eyes bored straight into hers.

"How long is it going to hurt this way?" he wanted to know.

Beholdenness surrounded her like the warm, soul-stirring waters of a baptismal fount. Heart thudding with reverence, she felt her own eyes well up. Overcome with gratitude to God for having heard their prayers…for having spared Bobby's eyesight, Dara wanted to praise Him on bended knee. But there would be time for that—a lifetime's worth—later. "Why don't we ring for the nurse," she suggested, biting back a sob, "see if maybe she can bring you something for the pain."

He turned back to his father. "Can we, Daddy?"

Noah closed his eyes, took a deep, shuddering breath, then looked at Dara. "He can see," he mouthed, smiling with relief. "He can see!"

She could only imagine how he must be feeling right now, if the realization that Bobby wasn't blind had stirred her so deeply.

"The doctor says that when you fell," Noah explained, his voice patient and kind, "you bruised your brain."

For a long time, no one said a word. The stillness was so complete the only sound in the room was the *tick, tick, tick* of Noah's wristwatch.

"When is it going to stop hurting?" he cried.

Dara patted the child's hand. "Soon, Bobby," she assured him, "soon. Before you know it, the swelling will go down, and you'll be your ornery old sel—"

"Don't," Noah interrupted, his soft voice suddenly hard edged, his face stern.

With a nod, Noah let Dara know he wanted to speak with her outside.

"Don't feed him a line of bunkum," came his harsh whisper when they reached the hall. "We're not out of the woods yet. It won't do him a bit of good, believing everything's gonna be right as rain. He needs to know it might get worse before—"

Dara stood as tall as her five-foot-three-inch frame would allow. Chin up and shoulders back, she glared at him. "What he *needs*," she hissed through clenched teeth, "is to be allowed to act like a little boy, because that's *exactly what he is*."

She watched the muscles of Noah's jaw flex, saw his

lips pull back in a taut, strained line. It was as though he'd drawn invisible boundaries around the boy, and she'd unwittingly crossed them. Her blatant statement had offended—no, it had *enraged*—him. This was not a man accustomed to being challenged, the somber look on his face said.

If you thought that was bad, wait till you hear what I have to say about your late wife.

In Dara's opinion, Angie and Bobby had been functioning like mini-adults more than long enough. She didn't know if their mother alone had required the stoic, straitlaced conduct or if their father had demanded it, as well, but right now, it didn't matter one whit to her. It was time someone spoke out on behalf of the Lucas children. You have no job, no family. What have you got to lose? she asked herself.

"Father?" Bobby called.

It broke Dara's heart to hear Bobby calling Noah "Father" again, and she would have said so, if Noah hadn't already turned on his heel and stomped back to his son's bedside.

She couldn't help but notice the child's clenched teeth and hands. He was making a Herculean effort to be brave…to gain *Father's* approval. You're lucky you and I aren't alone, she told Noah mentally, because you'd get such a piece of my mind that—

"Yes, son?"

They stood on either side of Bobby's bed, each holding a small, pale hand.

"I didn't mean to act like a baby," he said, sniffing. "I'll be good from now on. I promise. No more crying, 'cause I know you don't like it."

Noah would have needed to be blind not to see the boy's quavering lower lip, the agony in his eyes. She wanted to gather the dear little boy in her arms, tell him to cry at the top of his lungs, to rant and rave and stomp and shout if he felt like it, *to be a little boy!*

Dara reached across him, instead, gave Noah's shoulder a not-so-gentle shove. "Tell him!" she mouthed silently. "He's *not* a man!"

A shuddering sigh escaped Noah's lips as he slowly shook his head. Her rage seemed to have diffused his. "You're not being a baby, son. You're a brave, tough little guy, and I'm proud of you." And wrapping both arms around Bobby, Noah held him tight.

Father in heaven, she prayed, *give him the strength to be weak, for Bobby's sake....*

"Ah-h-h, son." Noah sighed raggedly, struggling to contain his tears.

A sob ached in her own throat when Noah did exactly what his son most needed him to do...

Wept.

Chapter Seven

Bobby had never gone to bed without a fight. At least, that's what Angie told Dara on Thanksgiving night, during their marathon "girl talk" session after the stint at the hospital; since his release, he'd been going upstairs without a word of protest, saying his prayers and drifting right off to sleep, almost as if he believed the accident had been a punishment of some sort.

And Dara had never missed a day's work, not once in eight years. But the Monday following the accident, she'd called the Centennial principal and informed him she wouldn't be coming back, explaining only that the Lucas children needed her more than the high school did.

"But...but you have three months to go before the semester break," he protested.

"What's the board gonna do, John?" she'd teased halfheartedly. "Fire me?"

He hadn't been happy about her pronouncement and said so, but agreed to make the necessary calls. A substitute would take her place until spring break, he said;

after that, thanks to budget cuts, the rest of the math teachers would have to divide Dara's students among themselves.

Ever since she'd heard about the reallocation of county funds that would phase out her job, she'd joked about the sedentary lifestyle she'd soon begin. Life would be anything *but* inactive once she began taking care of Angie and Bobby full-time, and she intended to do that full-time until the boy had completely recovered. After that, she'd volunteer at the elementary school, minister to the sick…and try to come to grips with what her father had done.

Money would be tight for a while, but if she watched how she spent her savings, she could last a year, maybe longer. For now, supporting herself was the least of her worries, because these next few days would be devoted to nursing Bobby back to health.

The neurologist had made it patently clear how close the boy had come to blindness, coma, brain damage. Once the doctor had explained that Bobby had hurt himself in a previous fall, Dara understood why, on the day the broom fell out of the pantry, Bobby had reacted so strangely to what should have been a minor bump on the head.

Dr. Tilley had said Bobby could go home, but only if, during the critical first twenty-four hours, he rested quietly. "Low lighting and as little noise as possible," the doctor had insisted. "And if he sleeps, someone has to wake him every sixty minutes, shine a flashlight into his eyes to make sure his pupils are constricting." They were to monitor him carefully throughout the next week, watching to see if Bobby could walk a straight line, hold down his meals, that he had no trouble focusing and that his memory of where objects were was intact. "Things are looking good," the doc had warned, "but it's too soon to celebrate."

Noah immediately agreed to reschedule his afternoon meetings so he could keep an eye on the boy. But Dara insisted he let *her* take care of the kids while Noah worked.

That had been four days ago.

Since then, first thing every morning, she'd been driving the three miles from her place in Valley Mede to his house in Font Hill, staying until the kids were sound asleep. It was starting to feel like home, this too-neat house of Noah's, from the big deck out back to the wraparound porch out front.

Dara had learned how to run Noah's multifunction computerized dishwasher and the tornadic vacuum cleaner. He'd shown her where he'd hidden the spare house key, taught her to operate the garage door opener by punching a secret code into the keypad.

And because her houseplants had more than doubled in size, blocking light—and, in warm weather, air from the open windows—she packed most of them into the back seat of her car and brought them to Noah's. They looked much better here than they had at her place, standing tall and lush in dark corners, brightening bookshelves, dangling from the mantel.

She'd brought over a few knickknacks, too—things she probably would have sold at a yard sale in the spring anyway—to further cozy up the place. The pink priscilla guest room curtains she'd been thinking of replacing now cheered Angie's room. And the spur-of-the-moment purchase she'd made at the church's Christmas bazaar—an antique quilt—didn't really match her decor, so she hung it over one arm of Noah's family room sofa.

If he noticed any of the things she'd done to warm the austere atmosphere of his house, he didn't show it. But he'd had a lot more than usual on his mind lately. And then, she'd been careful to keep her alterations and additions to a minimum, to make minor, insignificant changes. Because she certainly didn't want him thinking she was trying to run his life. That was the way he'd interpreted her tirade in Bobby's hospital room, and things hadn't been the same between them since.

She hadn't made her "let him be a boy" speech to hurt Noah. Rather, she'd made the statement totally on Bobby's behalf. And she'd remind herself of that every time the wounded, surprised look materialized on Noah's face.

Sadly, the expression seemed almost a permanent part of his demeanor these days, as if he blamed himself not only for Bobby's accident, but also for the fact that both his children had *for years* been behaving more like cute little robots than kids. Dara had spent enough time with the family before the boy's fall…had heard enough about the late great Mrs. Noah Lucas, to know it had been Francine, not Noah, who'd encouraged their virtually mechanical mannerisms.

But Francine had been dead for nearly four years. Why hadn't Noah sat those kids down before now, explained to them it was perfectly acceptable—*preferable*, even—to act their ages?

If she'd asked the question in the privacy of *her* mind, surely Noah had asked it of himself, dozens of times. She had to assume he'd asked it recently. What else could explain his dour mood, his quieter-than-usual demeanor, his inability to meet her eyes for more than a fraction of a second at a time. He was hurting, a fact that annulled her "Be Tough with Noah" plan.

Maybe she was reading too much into the hurt looks she believed she saw on Noah's face. Stop obsessing about it, she told herself. You may think he's hurting, and he probably hasn't given it a second thought.

Whether she was right or not really didn't matter. If he was suffering, she couldn't stand idly by and watch it. It was time for a confrontation. And tonight, the minute the kids were asleep, she'd go toe-to-toe with him if need be, until she could make him see it was never too late to change course, not when you had God on your side!

While she finished up the supper dishes, Noah tucked the kids in. Prior to the accident, the children were expected to be upstairs and ready for bed by eight-thirty; now, they didn't get started until then. A week ago, they could expect Noah to read them one story after they'd said their prayers; lately, they got at least two fairy tales apiece, following an overly long bedtime prayer and several trips to the bathroom—tiny paper cups leaving a water-drip trail from sink to bed—before he left them. And the odd thing was, Noah, not the children, had been the procrastinator.

She kept an ear cocked so she'd know when he came downstairs. When she heard his big feet thudding down the stairs, she stood in the kitchen doorway, a roll of tin foil in her hands. "Finished?"

"Yeah. Finally."

He could pretend he'd just survived yet another bedtime ordeal, but Dara knew better: Noah was afraid to let them out of his sight, even long enough to let them get a night's sleep.

Standing in the middle of the foyer, he pocketed both hands. "Need any help in there?"

"No, thanks." He'd been upstairs long enough for her to bake a pan of brownies, and she'd just stuck the foil-covered, nearly cooled treat into the microwave, when he descended the stairs. "I'm almost finished."

Grabbing his jacket from the hall tree, Noah opened the front door. "I'll be outside," he said, "in case the kids want me or anything."

It was becoming a habit, his walking in the cold, damp night alone. Right now, the temperature was thirty degrees and falling, and the weather bureau was predicting more snow. What had driven him out there this time?

Ever since she was a child, Dara had been enamored of wolves. When other little girls were dreaming of owning a pony, or becoming a ballerina, Dara had her nose stuck in a book, reading about *Canus lupus*. Even after all these years, Dara could almost quote her sources chapter and verse: one of the most intelligent beings in the animal kingdom, the big, beautiful beasts possessed well-honed instincts, sharp eyesight, keen hearing. But their most admirable trait, Dara believed, was devotion to family. Pack life was a carefully woven braid of togetherness that began with the collaborative nurturing of puppies, to group hunts that required the cooperation of all. Because they craved attention and affection, there were few things in nature sadder than a lone wolf. Whether alpha male disapproval or a forest fire separated him from the pack, the results were the same: overwhelming and heartbreaking yearning that could be measured by the sorrowful notes of his lonely howls.

Noah's behavior of late reminded her of a lone wolf;

he prowled the outskirts of the family, darting in now and then to test if acceptance was possible, bolting again when the threat of rejection seemed likely, even if only in his own mind. Did he blame himself for Bobby's condition? For neglecting to notice when the boy had experienced the initial injury? For missing the signs that something was not quite right with the child? Self-recrimination could be a powerful emotion if it was allowed to get out of control.

And Noah's was bordering on despair.

Dara heard the front door close quietly behind him. *Lord Jesus,* she prayed, closing her eyes, *help me to help Noah. He's wounded so badly that I think he's grown numb from the pain. Give me the right words, words that will help him remember You're there for him, words that will help him begin to heal.*

After cutting a brownie for each of them, she strode determinedly into the foyer, shrugged into her coat and went outside. He stood at the far end of the porch, bent over the banister, forearms leaning on the rail. "Hot from the oven," she said cheerily, walking toward him. "Your favorite."

In the faint sliver of moonlight slanting through the clouds, she could see the hint of a smile playing at the corners of his mustached mouth.

"I thought I smelled brownies baking while I was with the kids," he said, accepting one.

Dara plopped down on the top step, patted the space beside her. "Take a load off," she said, biting into her brownie.

Noah hesitated for a moment, as if uncertain whether or not he deserved even that minuscule bit of comfort. Sitting beside her, he stared straight ahead.

"This has been a strange winter, hasn't it?" She

laughed. "And it isn't even technically winter until December twenty-first."

Staring across the snowy lawn, he munched the brownie. "Tasty," he said.

"I memorized Grandma Mackenzie's recipe. She called it 'Lots of Brownies.' Too bad, though."

"Too bad?"

Dara nudged him with her shoulder. "They'll just end up on my hips."

Noah chuckled softly, his breath becoming tiny clouds that floated heavenward. "Like you have anything to worry about, skinny as you are."

"Thin, Noah," she scolded good-naturedly. "Ladies prefer trim or willowy or slender...*anything* but skinny."

"I'll make a note of it...Slim."

Even now, in his gloomy mood, his compliment had the power to make her blush. "It's awfully calm, considering what the weatherman said."

He turned slightly, looking into her face. "What did he say?"

"That we could get another six inches tonight."

"The calm before the storm," he observed, facing forward again.

Dara finished up her brownie, wadded up the napkin and stuffed it into her pocket. Holding her hand out, palm up, she waited until he gave her his. Hands deep in her napkin-lined pockets, she hunched her shoulders against the biting cold. "Noah?"

"Hmm."

"It isn't your fault."

Silence.

"Bobby's accident, I mean."

"I know what you mean."

"Well, it isn't."

She saw, rather than heard, his sigh, watched as its vapor was quickly carried away by an icy breeze.

Lord, be with me now. She searched her mind for a scripture verse to fit the moment: "A word fitly spoken is like apples of gold in pictures of silver." She waited, hoping for a sign of some sort, some divine guidance that would help her know what to do, what to say, to comfort Noah.

No such assistance came.

Suddenly, she remembered what he'd said about life at St. Vincent's, where people were always talking and a person was hard-pressed to get a moment's privacy. "I'm sorry, Noah," she said. "It wasn't very thoughtful of me, coming out here, interrupting you. You get so little time to be alone with your thoughts, especially these days, what with your work and trying to find time to be with the kids."

She made a move as if to get up, but his hand, clamped on her jacketed forearm, stopped her. "No, don't go." He met her eyes. "Unless…unless you're going in because you're cold."

Actually, she'd been shivering since she'd set foot outside. And with the weatherman predicting more snow… You don't want to get snowed in again, do you? she asked herself. But Dara smiled and shook her head. "I'm fine."

They sat side by side in companionable silence for a long time.

And then several scripture references flitted through her mind: "A fool's voice is known by a multitude of words"…"There is a time to keep silence, and a time to speak." The Bible verses had made no sense whatsoever when she'd memorized them as a child. But she understood them perfectly now. *So that's Your answer, Lord....*

She didn't know how much time had passed—five minutes? fifteen?—before Noah said, "I don't suppose you've given any more thought to my question."

"What question is that?"

"About us, about getting married."

Heart thundering, Dara swallowed. Except for Bobby's accident, she'd thought of little else. "Oh," she said. "That question." Because the boy's headache hadn't completely vanished yet, she'd more or less moved in to keep watch over him. Often, while driving home after a long day at the Lucases', Dara had mentally rewritten those highway signs advertising available housing from "If you lived here, you'd be home now" to "If you and Noah were married..."

As she silently debated the question of marrying Noah, she'd blamed her roller-coaster emotions on exhaustion, worry about Bobby, the shame and hurt and anger caused by what her father had done. And then the rational side of her brain would take over again. You can't marry a man who doesn't love you. And besides, he hasn't brought it up since the snowstorm, anyway.

May as well give it to him straight, she decided. It's the only way you can be sure this topic will never darken your doorstep again. She thought about where they were sitting, about where they'd been last time he brought up the idea of marriage. The subject will never darken *his* doorstep again.... "I'm an only child, y'know."

"So I've heard."

"My mom and dad were only children, too."

She could tell by the furrows in his brow that he had

no idea where she was going with this line of thought. "I can empathize with that last Mohican, since I'm the only Mackenzie left—at least, the only one of *my* Mackenzies left—so this whole business of preserving my father's reputation seems pointless. I mean, what sense does it make for you to replace the stolen money? It isn't as if I have to protect his mother or mine or—"

"What about the children you'll have someday? Don't you intend to tell them about their grandfather? If I put the two hundred thousand back, they'll never have to know. *No one* will have to know."

"I'll know," she replied dully. "Besides, I'm nearly thirty years old. What're—"

"You're going to have children. Plenty of them. God doesn't fill a woman to overflowing with natural-born nurturing tendencies unless He plans for her…plans to give her a passel of kids to spend all that love on."

"I used to believe that would happen." Another shrug. "But I was young and naïve then. I believed a lot of impossible things."

"Like what?"

"Oh, girl stuff mostly."

"Girl stuff?"

"In five or six years, you're going to know more about that than you ever dreamed possible!" She laughed. "Angie is going to turn into a teenager, and—"

Noah's groaning chuckle silenced her…temporarily.

"She's going to start talking about a handsome prince who'll come along and whisk her off to a pretty little cottage in the woods," she said wistfully, hands clasped beneath her chin, "where they'll raise a whole slew of little princes and Angies."

"You don't believe it anymore?"

"No."

"You sound awfully adamant."

"I lived my whole life believing my father was a prince." She gave a bitter little laugh. "And you know the old joke—'turns out he was just a frog.'"

"That's not really fair, is it?"

She thought about that for a minute, then shook her head. "Yeah, well," she said, "princes don't steal, now do they." It was more a statement than a question, and Dara hoped he'd see it that way, let the subject drop, once and for all.

"So, you're saying that just because your father made one mistake, you've given up all hope that the right man will come along, sweep you off your feet, give you that cottage and those kids."

One mistake? For all she knew, he had a whole secret life of crime going on behind her back. "That's what I'm saying."

Things weren't going the way she'd planned. Not even close. She'd intended to come out here, let him know that no one held him responsible for Bobby's accident. And what had happened, instead? *He* was comforting *her!*

Well, that wasn't entirely true. Noah was *trying* to console her, but his questions had, in effect, only served to make her more miserable than ever, because thinking about the futility of her fantasy was one thing, but putting it into words was something else entirely.

"Then there's nothing to keep you from marrying me, is there?"

She replayed the question in her mind.

"You said that night—when I first introduced the idea—that you'd couldn't marry a man you didn't love."

"That's right."

"Well, since you don't believe the man exists whom you *could* love, why not marry me?" He paused. "You'd have half the dream, at least."

"The cottage in the woods, you mean," she said, nodding toward the house.

"If you were my wife, everything I have would be ours," he corrected. "We could have a grand life."

"Yeah," she muttered, "two hundred grand."

"This isn't about the money, Dara."

"Isn't it?"

"No. It isn't." Clearing his throat, he continued. "Remember what I said about you that night when you got snowed in here?"

Dara hid her face in her hands. "I'm blushing just thinking about it."

"Well, I meant every word. I mean it all a hundred times more now. I choose my friends carefully," he repeated, "very carefully. And after what you've done for us these past few days, there isn't a doubt in my mind—there's no better friend in the world. And," he said, forefinger pressing into her jeans-clad knee, "there's *nobody* better for Angie and Bobby." He cleared his throat. "Especially Bobby."

You must really be losing it, Dara old girl, she thought, because this idea of his is starting to sound tempting. Very tempting.

"He needs a mom, now more than ever. The poor kid has always been scared of the dark." Almost as an afterthought, he said, "Did you know he slept with a night-light before...before..."

She grabbed his wrist, squeezed it tight. "It wasn't your fault, Noah! It was a freak accident. Period. So stop blaming yourself."

"It's more than the accident, and I think you know it."

Sidling closer, she linked her fingers with his.

"It's about everything…about the way I let Francine rule the roost, about the way I never questioned her disciplinary tactics. Don't get me wrong—she was a good woman, a good mother. I know how much she loved those kids, but—"

"She loved you, too. I've seen the proof dozens of times, in every picture in your family room."

"Yeah. I know."

Could have fooled me, Dara told him silently. "Can I ask you a question, Noah?"

"You can ask. But I don't seem to have very many answers these days."

He was referring to the accident, losing his wife, a hundred other things that seemed indefinable, unexplainable. "Why are you always so hard on yourself?"

"Hard on myself! If I was hard on myself, a lot of the things that have happened…well, they wouldn't have happened."

"What are you talking about?"

"I always figured it was my duty to become a part of the rat race…to pay the bills, y'know? And it was Francine's job to take care of…of practically everything else. 'Man must work from sun to sun,'" he quoted, "'but woman's work…'"

Noah blew a stream of air through his teeth. "I was 'Mr. Important Working Man.' Didn't have time to drive the kids to birthday parties and piano lessons." He grunted. "I always had time for golf outings and fishing trips. Had plenty of time to make use of my Orioles season tickets."

Another grunt. "God set it all in action thousands

of years ago. He intended for *man* to be the head of the house. And what did I do? Handed the job off to Francine. That's what.''

A silent moment ticked by. "Wasn't fair. Wasn't right.''

"Maybe it wasn't right,'' Dara agreed, "but from everything I've heard about Francine, it sounds to me as if she *enjoyed* being in charge.''

"She *was* pretty good at it,'' he admitted, a smile of fond remembrance collapsing into a shudder of embarrassment.

"And you were pretty good at supporting your family. Just look at this beautiful house. And what about the home you had in Pennsylvania? I've seen photographs...it was a virtual mansion!''

She rambled on. "The kids told me about the fun family vacations and all those luxurious, romantic places you took Francine, just the two of you. The way I hear it, she knows London as well as any Brit! And you bought her nearly every piece of expensive jewelry, every fur, every fancy car, she ever asked for, too. You couldn't be in two places at one time, Noah. How were you supposed to provide everything she said she wanted without working long and hard?''

He chuckled softly. "Listen to you, defending me as though you're my mom or something. Do you see what I mean? You're a natural-born mother.'' Then, suddenly serious, Noah shook his head. "But making excuses for my bad behavior doesn't change anything.''

"*What* bad behavior? You were a model husband. You're the perfect father.''

"Oh, yeah? Well, if I'm so perfect, how come my kids are so busy trying to be perfect that they've forgotten how to be kids? They get so little practice acting their age that when they *do* cut loose a little, they don't know how to behave. *That's* why Bobby never told me when he fell—''

She gave his arm a gentle shake. "Stop it. I won't listen to another word of this nonsense. You did the best you could under the circumstances. No one, not even God, could expect more of you than that."

"*I* expect more. A whole *lot* more."

Without warning, he turned, gripped her upper arms. "Say you'll marry me, Dara. I know I can be the father those kids deserve…with you at my side."

"You're the father they deserve right now."

Moonlight, reflected in his pale eyes, glittered like hard diamonds. He didn't believe her, she knew, as evidenced by his furrowed brow and taut lips.

Noah had told her all about his days at St. Vincent's. "I didn't deserve a family," he'd said, "so when Angie and Bobby came along, I just assumed they were God's gifts to Francine." His wife, he'd said, had earned them, because unlike him, she'd never committed a wrong in her life.

She made you believe you were good enough for her only when you were doling out gifts and trips and attention in hearty doses. And she turned your kids into walking, talking robots. How right was that? Dara thought, but said nothing.

Pain shimmered in his eyes, and Dara bit her lower lip, praying for God to show her a way to relieve his agony.

And then it came to her.

She could marry him, and just as he'd suggested, be his helpmate. Then, day by day, she could show him proof that he was—and always had been—a wonderful, loving father, a wonderful loving *man.*

And why not? Her Prince Charming wasn't coming. Not now. Not ever. Because, as she'd told Noah, no such man existed. So why *not* marry him, do something honorable and worthwhile with the rest of her life? Because he'd been right: she *had* been good for Bobby and Angie, and she could be good for Noah, too. The Lord knows they've been good for you, she admitted; she'd never felt more wanted, more needed, in her life.

"All right, Noah," she murmured. "I'll marry you."

He looked at her for a moment, as if unable to believe she'd said yes. When he pulled her to him, she felt him tremble. "Do you mean it?" he whispered into her ear.

Her arms went around him as if she'd been born to it, and the truth spilled from her lips. "I've never meant anything more."

Noah held her at arm's length, studied her face. "You won't be sorry," he said, smiling wider than she'd ever seen on his handsome face. "I'll take good care of you. I promise."

Tears sparkled in his eyes. Caused by joy? she wondered. Or regret at having been forced by circumstance to replace his beloved Francine with the daughter of a common thief? It didn't matter. "I know you'll take care of me, Noah. I'll take good care of you, too."

He threw back his head and laughed. "As if I didn't know that already. Why, you've already spoiled me rotten in just this past week."

"You ain't seen nothin' yet, Mr. Lucas," she said. "I'm going to take such good care of you and Angie and Bobby you'll wonder how you ever did without me!"

After a moment, he said, "I'm wondering that already."

Something had happened as she'd looked into his shining, damp eyes, something that made her realize there was more, much more involved here than agreeing to this marriage of convenience.

She wanted to do all those things for Noah, in part because he deserved them, in part because she'd suddenly begun to hope that by doing them, she might be able to earn his love.

He hadn't ridden into her life on a great white mount, and maybe his armor did have a few dings in it, but he was her prince nonetheless.

Chapter Eight

Unceremoniously dropping the big dress box onto her bed, Dara kicked off her shoes and stepped into her slippers. According to the digital alarm, it was nine-thirty. Feels more like midnight, she groused, heading for the kitchen.

She filled the teapot, and as she waited for the water to boil, Dara sorted through the day's mail. She set aside the bills—one from the power company, another from the telephone carrier—and without so much as a glance at the assorted catalogs and sales brochures set them aside.

She tore open a few envelopes, had a cursory look inside. The public access television station wanted a donation. A candidate running for the House of Delegates wanted her vote. Two charities wanted her help in distributing pamphlets. A telemarketer wanted her assistance in performing a survey.

The plants wanted water, the furniture a good dusting and the carpets a thorough vacuuming. Even the

teapot wanted something from her, and she turned off
the burner to still its insistent whistle.

She'd been spending every day at the Lucases', making sure Dr. Tilley's orders for Bobby's care were followed to the letter. Under her conscientious, loving attention, he healed, and by the end of that first week,
he was back at school, headacheless and carefree. Sens-
ing he'd progress more quickly if she didn't hover over
him, Dara took it upon herself to organize the linen
closet, straighten the pantry shelves, rearrange the furniture in the family room so that no matter where a
person sat, the fire in the woodstove and the television
set could be viewed without inducing a stiff neck. Between her twice-hourly checks on the boy, she'd polished the hardwood floors. Shampooed the carpets and
upholstery. Waxed the kitchen cupboards. Washed the
curtains.

On the way to their house in the morning, she
stopped at a twenty-four-hour market for groceries. On
the way back to her place, she'd dropped off Noah's
suits and sport coats at the dry cleaner's.

She did all this because any day now, his address
would be hers, too, a fact that compelled Dara to turn
the big, newly built Victorian into a home for the four
of them.

Two days and counting, she thought, spooning sugar
into her mug. Two days until you'll be Mrs. Noah Lucas....

She tossed a tea bag on top of the sugar, drowned
both with hot water and stirred, oblivious to the clink
of metal against ceramic. The cinnamony scent of the
tea wafted into her nostrils. Spicy apple had always
been her mother's favorite flavor....

Smiling, she dropped the soggy tea bag into the trash

can, remembering it was one of her mother's many habits, the worst of which—according to Jake—was her tendency to leave cold, wet tea bags on the countertop. It was the main point of contention between her parents. Actually, it was the *only* point of contention she could recall between them, though she supposed there were some issues they worked out in private.

She knew this much: whatever bound them together, heart to heart, that was what she wanted in her own marriage. Is that possible, she wondered, when you're not marrying for love? And this is a marriage of convenience. Isn't it?

Sighing, Dara remembered that those tea bags were the first things her father had talked about the morning after her funeral. "Lord," he'd said, his voice soft and wistful, brown eyes misting with unshed tears, "what I wouldn't give to have another cold, wet tea bag to complain about...."

"I miss her, too," Dara had said, hugging him.

Dara sipped her tea. Seems like only yesterday; could it really have been two years ago?

Glancing at the picture on the mantel of her parents on one of their many trips to London, tears filled her eyes. I miss you, too, Daddy, she thought. Oh, how I miss you....

Dara carried her mug into the bedroom, placed it on the nightstand and stared at the shiny pink box on her bed. Inside it, wrapped in red tissue paper, lay the outfit she'd wear to her wedding. It was nothing fancy, just a simple two-piece suit, more than adequate to exchange vows in the pastor's office.

The pastor's office, she thought, grimacing.

She thought she'd accepted the fact that none of her dreams were going to come true. No Prince Charming.

No church filled with friends and relatives and flowers lining the altar steps. There'd be no white runner to lead her to the altar. Worst of all, she had no father to walk her down the aisle, no mother to turn in that first pew, teary-eyed and smiling, as Dara took her place beside her husband-to-be.

The stark mental picture reminded her of the last conversation she'd had with her mother.

During Anne's last weeks—because she hadn't been strong enough to do much else—Dara stopped by every evening on her way home from work, carrying a collection of slick fashion magazines in her arms. She'd lie beside her mother on the big rented hospital bed in her parents' room. Heads and shoulders touching, giggling and rolling their eyes, they leafed through page after page of the latest fads.

They played Scissors, Paper, Rock to determine who'd keep the perfume samples—a practice that soon had Anne's nightstand drawer filled to overflowing. Critiquing hairdos and makeup and commenting on the ultrathin models was a fun, stress-free activity that always seemed to brighten her mother's wan features.

On the very afternoon of her mother's death, Dara had tucked a brides' magazine in with the others. If she could have predicted—as they made their way through the stack—that looking at white gowns and headdresses would make Anne cry, she'd have slipped it from the stack and hidden it for sure.

"Now, don't get me wrong," Anne had said, sniffing and blotting her eyes on a corner of the starched white sheet. "I love being married to your father. Always have. But if I had it to do over again, I would have listened to your grandmother. I would have exercised a little patience and waited for that nice church wedding I'd always dreamed about.'' Her voice, wispy and weak, faded as she struggled for each breath.

Dara had tried to convince her mother to conserve her energy, but telling the story seemed to calm her more than silence could have.

''Your dad was a lieutenant in those days.'' Anne had smiled serenely. ''A navy test pilot,'' she whispered, closing her eyes. ''Oh, how handsome he was in his flight suit.'' She sighed. ''The minute we learned he'd be shipping out for six months of sea duty, we decided to tie the knot, so I could start setting up house while he was gone. We ended up exchanging vows in the pastor's office—me in my Sunday best, your dad in his dress uniform.''

They'd gone through it so many times it could have been a one-act play. ''But, Mom,'' Dara said, as if rehearsed, ''if you *had* waited, you would have had six months less with Dad.''

Nodding weakly, her mother closed her eyes. ''That's true,'' she'd whispered. ''And every moment counts, especially now, doesn't it?''

Her mother had gripped her hand then, forcing Dara to meet her eyes. ''Oh, sweet girl, how I wish I could be at *your* wedding.''

''I'm just a few years shy of thirty, Mom,'' she'd teased halfheartedly, ''there isn't much chance—''

''It'll *happen*.'' Anne's voice, strong and sure, belied her condition. ''You'll see. Before you know it, when you least expect it, the man of your dreams will come into your life and—'' She'd giggled softly, squeezing Dara's hand. ''Wear something pretty and feminine to your wedding. Do it for me, okay?''

Dara pushed the tissue paper aside, exposing the suit. Pretty and feminine enough for you, Mom? She leaped from the bed, pressed the jacket to her torso and did a slow pirouette in front of her mirror. This wasn't at all what you had in mind, was it? She could be certain, because Anne had opened the brides' magazine and dog-eared a center page. "*This* is the kind of dress I want you to wear on your oh-so-special day," she'd gushed.

Dara laid the jacket gently atop its matching skirt and stepped into her closet. There, in a discarded boot box on the lower shelf, lay that very magazine. She opened it to the page her mother had marked, flopped onto the bed beside her suit and smiled thinly.

The gown was made of creamy-white satin, and its sweetheart neckline and pirate sleeves were trimmed in tiny pearls. The train began at the tightly petaled rosette at the small of the waist and cascaded to the floor like a silken waterfall that came to rest in a puddle and stretched out for fifteen feet. The veil, made of dozens of yards of finely woven lace, gave a cloudlike illusion as it floated to the floor from the pearl-encrusted tiara.

Closing the periodical, Dara lay on her stomach, fingers skimming across the chalk-white wool. Tastefully elegant, the suit fitted as if it had been sewn exclusively for her. Its scalloped neckline and sleeves had been trimmed with tiny, opalescent buttons. She'd bought a narrow-brimmed milk-white hat to go with it, and after opening the round hatbox, Dara poked her finger into its stiff, open-weave veil that would hide her face until that magic moment.

"It isn't what you wanted for me, Mom," she whispered, folding the tissue over the suit, "but it'll do…for the kind of ceremony we've planned."

Planned? Ha! she thought, rolling onto her back. One hand lay under her pillow; the other rested atop the tissue-covered wedding suit. The only thing planned about this wedding is that there will be a wedding at all!

She had hoped, once she'd agreed to become his wife, that Noah would make time somewhere in his schedule to talk about their future. Should she arrange a small reception at his house, so he could entertain employees and clients? Who would witness the exchange of vows in Pastor Williams's cramped little office? Would there be a honeymoon?

He hadn't discussed any of the details of life after the ceremony, either, except to say that since the children had grown so accustomed to their spacious house on Kingsway Drive, it would be best if Dara moved in with them, instead of the other way around.

It meant having to sell almost everything.

There was a bright side to that dark cloud: use the proceeds from the sale of her parents' house and the condo to pay back the money Dad stole. She had no intention of letting Noah right her father's wrong. What kind of life would they have if they started out he the great and generous "giver of things" and she the needy "taker."

It wouldn't be easy selling the two-bedroom condo she'd bought with a down payment from her first-year teaching, but it'd be a whole lot less painful than seeing the For Sale sign go up in front of the rambling manor house where she'd grown up.

Soon after her father died, Dara had packed up her parents' personal belongings and put them in storage. Things that didn't fit into her own condo had been given to friends or sold at ridiculously low prices to couples just starting out.

Her dad had been gone six months now, and she

hadn't been in the house, not once, since opening it to let a young engaged couple take a look at the living room suite. The Victorian antiques Dara's mother had collected over the years were worth easily ten times what the lovebirds paid for them. Remembering how her father felt about the mustard-colored velvet divan and two ornate, blue-green brocade side chairs made it easy to let them go so cheaply. "This place is starting to look like the back of a tinker's wagon!" he'd complain. But her mother's love for antiques outweighed his need for a simpler life, as evidenced by her continual additions to the outrageous collection.

Dara had been left with mixed feelings as she'd sold off the pieces that had so distressed her father—and so pleased her mother. She had easily found people whose appreciation for the gaudy stuff matched her mother's own. She'd let it all go—lead-crystal lamps with silk shades, baroque candlesticks, sateen throw pillows, the elaborately carved cherry tables—for a song. "In your honor, Dad," she'd whispered, watching the happy couple drive off pulling their overflowing rented trailer.

She'd decorated her own bright, airy rooms with an eclectic mix of plainness and color. Bright area rugs lay on well-scrubbed hardwood floors. Cream camel-backed sofas and chairs flanked the fireplace. Terra-cotta lamps with parchment shades sat on maple Shaker tables. Indoor trees and houseplants in brass kettles and wicker urns formed a natural curtain between her world and the bustling street outside. And it was all a one-of-a-kind backdrop for her lifelong collection of wolf figurines.

Except for the wolves, she would have to leave it all behind. But what did it matter? She had her memories, didn't she?

"Oh, Daddy," Dara whispered as tears filled her eyes, "if only I had known...."

Known what? That his trip to England would kill him? That he'd be accused of a despicable crime afterward?

If he hadn't stolen that money, Noah would never have proposed in the first place.

She'd been telling herself the only reason she'd agreed was that Noah needed her to keep another accident like the one that had nearly blinded Bobby from happening. But Dara knew in her heart that wasn't true; he'd been doing a fine job taking care of his kids without her.

But if not for the missing two hundred thousand, if not to take care of the kids, then why *had* she agreed to marry him?

Dara gingerly fingered the pearly buttons on her wedding suit. Admit it, she thought, you want to marry him...because you love him.

Noah stood in Angie's doorway, hands pocketed, and watched her sleep. The hallway light slanted into her room, illuminating her pixie-ish face. She'd pulled the covers up tight under her chin, tiny fingertips sticking out as she clutched at the satiny trim of her fuzzy pink blanket. She tried so hard, during her waking hours, to behave like a grown-up, but asleep, Angie was every bit a child...innocent, sweet, very much in need of a mother's protection and care.

Soon, he told her silently, soon you'll have it. Quietly, he pulled her door, leaving it open just enough so that he'd hear her if she called out in her sleep.

He walked down the carpeted hall and stepped softly into Bobby's room. As usual, the boy had kicked off his covers and lay on his side, hugging his knees to his chest. Noah eased the covers up carefully, so as not to wake him. The boy was safe and sound and sleeping peacefully. There was no reason to linger.

But he couldn't seem to make himself leave. He'd come so close, paralyzingly close, to losing him.

Noah reached out, brushed Bobby's blond hair back from his forehead. The young boy stirred and, without opening his eyes, murmured "Daddy?" in a small, soft voice.

On his knees beside the bed, Noah held the boy to his chest. "I'm here, son," he whispered, lips pressed to the boy's temple. "I'm here."

He waited a moment to hear what Bobby wanted. A drink of water? A trip to the bathroom? A second bed-time story, perhaps?

But he slept on, deep and sound, and Noah realized he hadn't awakened at all. Rather, he'd called, in his dream state, from an honest place where the man who'd been entrusted with the care of his little body and his big heart was, simply, "Daddy."

He laid Bobby back on the pillow, tucked the covers under his chin, kissed his cheek. "Sweet dreams, son." He sighed. "I love you."

"Love you," Bobby mumbled into his pillow.

If you hug him again, you'll wake him for sure, Noah thought. And so, regretfully, he got to his feet, and walked from the room.

In the family room, Noah settled into his chair, laid the Bible on his lap, let it fall open at will. "I am my beloved's and my beloved is mine," he read from the Song of Solomon. "Thou art beautiful."

Like Dara....

He closed the Holy Book. This time when he opened

it, it fell to Exodus: "If he came in by himself, he shall go out by himself; if he were married, then his wife shall go out with him."

She'll stand beside you, really stand beside you, forever....

"Husbands, love your wives, even as Christ also loved the church, and gave himself for it."

I'll be good to her, he promised himself.

"It is not good for man to be alone...."

And it isn't. He knew, because he'd been alone as a child, alone in his marriage, alone after Francine died. He'd had enough of it to last several lifetimes. But with Dara, it would be different. He hadn't felt alone since meeting her; with Dara, he'd never be alone again.

He closed the Good Book, thumb tracing the gold cross emblazoning the brown leather cover. Two more days, he thought, a slow smile spreading over his face. Just two more days.

He wondered what she'd wear. Sensible shoes? A perky little hat? A kicky, knee-length dress? Surely not a billowing white gown and a long flowing veil like Francine had worn. No, not for a wedding in Williams's musty office. It seemed terribly unfair, because Dara was a beautiful woman, inside and out, and she deserved to be married in satin and lace, surrounded by fresh-cut flowers, in a church filled with friends.

He remembered that night in his family room, when she'd said in her straightforward way: "My father gets his good name back, you'll get a chief cook and bottle washer and your kids get a substitute mother. What's in it for me?"

Noah hadn't known what to say then. But he knew what had been in his mind. He loved her, more than he had ever thought it possible for a man to love a woman, and he'd spend the rest of his days finding ways to prove it.

His smile grew as an idea began forming in his mind. If all went well, he'd start proving it on their wedding day. And it would be just the kind of wedding gift she deserved.

In bold black felt-tip marker, the sign printed on a cardboard shirt-backer said Please Use Church Entrance.

Tightening her hold on the umbrella's hook-shaped handle, Dara stood at the door to Pastor Williams's office and huffed her exasperation. Now she'd have to traipse along the narrow path that hugged the complex…in the driving snow.

Now, really, she asked herself, why are you surprised? Nothing about your life has been right. Not since Mom died.

Things had only gone downhill from there…her father's first heart attack, his death, Dara's discovery of his crime. She'd lost her job, too, and now she was on her way to marry a man who didn't—and likely *never* would—love her, since he so obviously still loved the wife he'd lost years earlier. A terrifying, almost smothering, thought haunted her, one she'd tried her best to keep at bay: How do I compete with a woman he considers to be perfect?

The thunderstorm that blew through during the night had knocked out the electricity in her neighborhood. Dara guessed she must have fallen asleep sometime around 4:00 a.m. When she awoke again, the red numerals of the alarm clock said 6:42. A quick check of her watch had told her it was 8:58. She had exactly forty-seven minutes to shower, put on her makeup, fix her hair, get into her suit and make the fifteen-minute drive to the church. Because the ceremony—if a quickie exchange of "I do's" could be called a ceremony—would begin at ten. If she didn't want to be late for her own wedding, there wasn't a moment to lose. She'd skipped breakfast and rushed around, before leaving the house with a full ten minutes to spare.

But there had been a fender bender at the corner, blocking traffic, and she'd been forced to take the long way around. Despite hitting every red light, and the fact that folks were driving more slowly than usual because of the snow, Dara still managed to make it to the church five minutes ahead of schedule.

But now this little sidetrack.

The weight of it all descended without warning, and fighting tears, Dara ducked into a recessed doorway. *I was a well-behaved child, wasn't I?* she asked God. *Didn't I follow the letter of Your law? Wasn't I an obedient believer?* Was this to be her reward, then, for having lived a life of doing the right thing—being forced to forgo a real church wedding she and her mom had dreamed of…without family and friends, without flowers, without music?

She recited a verse from Philippians: "'Do all things without murmurings and disputings.'" Taking a deep breath, she recalled an even more appropriate line from Psalms: "O my God, my soul is cast down within me; therefore I will remember Thee.…"

And in the remembering, her father's favorite Bible passage came to mind: "God is faithful, who will not suffer you to be tempted above that ye are able; but will with the temptation also make a way to escape, that ye may be able to bear it."

Noah may never love her, but his children would.

And that'll be enough, she thought, blotting her eyes with a crumpled tissue taken from her coat pocket. I'll be the best wife and mother I know how to be, and by the grace of God, it'll be enough!

The heels of her winter-white shoes clicked over the brick path leading from the pastor's office to the wide double doors of the church. In the vestibule, once she'd closed the umbrella and hung up her coat, Dara looked at her wristwatch. Two minutes to ten.

She glanced toward the front of the church and saw him standing on the altar, feet shoulder width apart, hands clasped behind his back. He'd worn a coal-black suit, a starched white shirt, a silvery blue tie that, even from this distance, she knew matched his eyes exactly. Bobby stood to his right, Angie to his left. Well, she told herself, there they are…your new family.

Her *family!*

Heart swelling and throbbing with joy and over-whelming love for them—for *all* of them—she was powerless to control her emotions. She bowed her head, praying that the veil of her hat would hide her tears.

She met Noah's eyes, and he gave a slight nod, as if granting permission for her to join them as Angie, wearing a frilly, shin-length dress of deep red velvet, half ran, half skipped down the center aisle. Only then did Dara notice the white runner skimming the carpeted floor.

"Pastor Williams says when I get back up to the altar rail," Angie whispered, "I'm supposed to give you something."

Feelings of self-pity were quickly forgotten as Dara looked into the girl's wide, expectant eyes. "A surprise?"

Nodding, Angie said from behind all eight fingertips, "I'll give you a hint. It's red and white."

When Dara looked up, she saw the pastor's usual tightly controlled smile. He wasn't wearing a suit, as she'd expected. Instead, he'd donned the satiny white robe that he reserved for baptisms and confirmations...and weddings. He stepped aside and flipped a switch, then waved her forward.

"C'mon," Angie said, taking Dara's hand. "It's time."

Chapter Nine

"Time?" Dara asked, voice trembling nearly as badly as her hands. "Time for what?"

"Time to get *married*, silly!"

Married.

Dara's heart thundered in reaction to the finality of it. If you walk up that aisle, she thought, staring at the white runner, there's no turning back. If you say "I do" to Noah up there in a few minutes, four lives are going to change forever.

The thought reminded her of that afternoon last week, when Noah had insisted she be present when he sat the children down, and explained.

"Next Saturday," he'd said, hands folded on the kitchen table, "Miss Dara and I will be getting married. What do you say to that?"

The kids had exchanged puzzled glances, then stared silently at their somber-faced father. Bobby spoke first. "Does that mean she'll be your new wife?"

Noah had nodded.

He gave it a moment's thought, then shrugged one

shoulder. "Sounds like a good idea to me." Then, almost as an afterthought, he looked at Angie. "Isn't it?"

She heaved an exasperated sigh. "Of course it is. If they're married, she can stay with us *all* the time, instead of just during the day." She aimed her wizened gaze at Dara, tiny worry lines furrowing her brow. "May I ask a question?"

Smiling, Dara laid her hand atop Angie's. "Sure."

"Will you...will you be sleeping in Father's room or the guest room?"

Fact was, she and Noah had never discussed it, so Dara didn't know how to answer. She'd blinked and swallowed and clasped her hands tightly in her lap. "I—I, ah, I'm not—"

"She'll sleep in my room," Noah interrupted, his frown deepening. "Wives are supposed to sleep with their husbands."

"Does it say that in the Bible?" Bobby wanted to know.

Noah had coughed. Cleared his throat. "I'm sure it says something like that somewhere in the Good Book."

Another confused look between brother and sister had made Dara wonder if perhaps they, like their father, viewed her as a housekeeper, a cook, a glorified baby-sitter.

Then, grinning, Bobby met her eyes. "Good luck," he'd said, "'Cause Father sounds like a growly bear when he snores."

Angie giggled her agreement. "He hogs the blankets, too."

Their innocent warnings had caused his cheeks to flush slightly. "All right," he broke in. "Get your chores finished so we can see that movie you've been talking about all week.''

The recorded strains of the "Wedding March," wafting from the overhead speakers, interrupted Dara's reverie. Angie's gentle tugging propelled her forward, and she allowed herself to be led down the white-carpeted aisle. Another couple must be getting married when we're through here, she thought as she passed huge white satin bows and flowers that hung from every pew. Funny, but I don't remember reading about a wedding in last week's bulletin, she added as she neared the altar that was alight with the multicolored blooms of daisies, chrysanthemums, and roses.

So many questions ping-ponged in her mind—what other couple would become man and wife today and how had the pastor arranged permission for her and Noah to make use of their flowers, their decorations, their music?—that she barely knew how she made it from vestibule to altar. Later, Angie would get a well-deserved hug for being such a fastidious guide. For now, it was all Dara could do to keep her knees from knocking.

Pastor Williams lifted his chin and, opening his gilded prayer book to a page marked by a purple satin ribbon, said in a booming voice that echoed in the near-empty church, "I didn't think you'd mind a slight change in plans."

Dara read the mischief in his eyes, the impish grins on the kids' faces, and deduced that a conspiracy was afoot.

"Since the youngsters had to be here anyway," Williams continued, "I thought it might be nice if they participated in the ceremony. Any problem with that?"

Noah hesitated a moment before saying, "Makes sense to me. I only wish *I'd* thought of it."

Williams looked at Dara.

"What's about to happen here will affect them for the rest of their lives," she said, glancing in Noah's direction. "I think it's only fitting and proper that we make them part of...things."

"Good, good!" Clearing his throat, Williams flipped another switch, which silenced the music. "Angie will be your maid of honor," he said to Dara, "and Noah, Bobby will be your best man."

Maid of honor. Best man. It was happening. It was really happening!

Dara and Noah looked at each other for an instant before he averted his gaze. "That'll be fine. Just fine."

"Now, then," Williams said with a nod. "Angie...?"

She lifted her shoulders and smiled. "Oops! I almost forgot!" And tiptoeing behind the pulpit, she retrieved a huge bouquet. "Here's your surprise," Angie announced, handing it to Dara.

"Wh-why thank you, sweetie," Dara stammered, accepting the flowers. Almost instinctively, she lifted them to her face, inhaled their honeyed perfume. "But... But when...? Where—"

"Now, then," the pastor interrupted, "let us begin."

Was it Dara's imagination, or was the pastor speaking in an unusually loud voice?

Noah took his place at Dara's right, and as if rehearsed, Bobby stood beside him. Angie got into line on Dara's left as the doors swooshed open, admitting no less than half the congregation. As the parishioners—some Dara had known all her life—took their seats, Carl Rhodes scurried along the wall, tripod in one hand, photo bag in the other, a clunking necklace of cameras dangling around his neck.

"I'll just be a minute," he said in a quietly apologetical voice as he snapped a 35 mm into place atop the tripod. "There. That's got it. You can start now."

Flowers. Music. Friends. Dara didn't know how to explain that the wedding of her dreams was unfolding all around her. *And to think that a few minutes ago, you were standing in a wet doorway, feeling sorry for yourself,* she scolded inwardly. *Why me?* she had demanded of the Almighty.

Now she knew, and the knowledge brought tears of sweet, grateful joy to her eyes.

"No good thing will He withhold from them that walk uprightly," she recited mentally. "Praise ye the Lord. O give thanks unto the Lord...!"

In the week before the wedding, while Noah was at work and the children were in school, Dara had made arrangements to put her condo and her parents' place on the market. And box by box, bit by bit, she'd moved her personal belongings into Noah's house.

There were little reminders of her personality scattered through the rooms now, from the cookie sheets in the kitchen to the sunflower-covered ironing board in the laundry room. A black wrought-iron floor lamp that had been her paternal grandmother's now stood beside Noah's chair in the family room. Her father's pipe collection sat on a shelf in the dining room hutch, her mother's Wedgwood teapot beside it.

When she'd pulled open the double doors to the brightly lit closet in the master bedroom, Dara found that Noah had cleared the entire right side for her things. She had a long rod for hanging her dresses and pants, and two shorter ones for skirts and jackets. On the back wall, built-in cubbies would hold as many as thirty pairs of shoes. Above it, there were hooks for belts and scarves, and shelves for sweaters. On one side of the shoe cubby stood a tall lingerie chest; on the other, a three-drawer dresser.

She'd gone into his closet to hang freshly laundered and pressed shirts; why hadn't she noticed all this before? *And you were worried about crowding him!* Dara doubted that even after she'd put away every article of clothing and every accessory she owned, her side of the closet would still be half-empty. She could shop until doomsday, and likely not fill it.

Not that she had the money for shopping sprees, being out of a job and all.

And speaking of work, Dara hadn't given much thought to whether or not she'd continue teaching. Her preference was to be a full-time mom to Angie and Bobby, at least until they adjusted to her as their step-mother. She supposed if the subject came up, Noah would agree. At least, she hoped he would agree.

And then there was the matter of fulfilling her life-long dream…something Dara had been praying about almost since the night she'd gotten stuck at Noah's because of the snow.

For now, though, there were other, far more pressing, things to worry about.

The sleeping arrangements, for starters.

Though it had been on her mind—frequently—the issue hadn't come up. If not for Angie's innocent, inquisitive question, Dara probably still wouldn't know where she'd be bunking down.

Now, as she tucked shoes into their cubes, Dara could see the bed in the long narrow mirror at the back of the closet. He'd haphazardly slung a king-size hunter-green comforter over the pillows; a corner of the maroon blanket's satiny trim dragged the floor. Though he'd hung room-darkening shades, there were no curtains at the windows. And not a knickknack in sight on the oak dressers or matching nightstands. One clay-pot lamp stood on the table to the left of the bed. He prefers the left, she thought, and that's good, because I like the right.

Dozens of times, she'd dusted the alarm clock on the table near the lamp. It had always fascinated her, the way the black-numbered white tabs flopped into place with an audible *click*. Eight-thirty-nine, it said now.

Dara sighed. She'd heard the children come upstairs a few minutes ago to start getting ready for bed. If things went as usual, Noah would soon join them. Would she be invited to participate in their nighttime ritual? Or would they prefer to keep it private, something to be shared by the three Lucases? Much as she'd like to fuss over them once they'd climbed into bed, she wanted only what was best for them. If that meant she must keep her distance, she'd learn to deal with the hurt.

The clock *clicked* again. Eight-forty now.

What time did Noah turn in for the night? she wondered. Before the eleven o'clock news? Afterward? Was he the type who showered at night or first thing in the morning? Except for the time she'd gotten snowed in and the night that Bobby went to the hospital, Dara had never been in the Lucas house past nine.

Oh, she'd made many a nighttime trip to the second floor during the week following Bobby's recovery, but only to help the kids get into their pajamas. Never had she ventured to the other end of the hall, where the door to Noah's room stood slightly ajar.

Telling herself it was a necessary means to an end, she'd never had any trouble barging in there during the daylight hours. Sheets must be changed, carpets must be vacuumed, furniture must be dusted...

There had been that one time, though, when she'd been on her hands and knees, trying to reach a balled-up sock that had fallen from her laundry basket and rolled under Noah's bed. It had been obvious, when he stopped dead in his tracks in the doorway, that he hadn't expected to find her there, head and shoulders hidden by the dust ruffle, because the tune he'd been whistling died a quick and sudden death and the smile on his face vanished like a rabbit in a magician's act.

"What're you doing?" he'd grumped as she got to her feet. And when she told him, he'd scrubbed a hand over his reddened face and stomped from the room, muttering something about people being more careful and paying more attention to what was going on around them. His tirade hadn't made a bit of sense, but Dara had more or less gotten used to his mood swings. The inconsistency of his disposition sometimes baffled her, and that day, she'd likened him to the dark, brooding hero in *Jane Eyre*.

The clock *clicked* again, putting an end to her moment of respite from the "who's sleeping in my bed" quandary. Any time now, she'd have to unpack one of the nighties she'd just folded into the lingerie chest; sooner or later she'd have to scrub her face at one of the two sinks in the lavish master bath; eventually, she'd have no choice but to climb into that—

"Dara?"

She lurched at the sound of his voice and, clutching

a hand to her throat, took a breath to steady her nerves. "In here," she called.

He joined her in the closet. "Getting settled, I see," he said, smiling stiffly.

She nodded. "There's one more box to unpack, and it's—"

"The big one in the foyer, marked 'Wolves'?"

Another nod.

"I cleared a space for you on the mantel."

The mantel? It was all she could do to suppress a laugh. "Noah," she began, "I've been collecting wolves since I was ten years old. At last count, there were forty-seven of them." The mantel, her comment implied, would never hold them all. Dara got to her feet, closed the lingerie drawer. "Don't worry, though, I'll find places for my 'pets' that won't be too obtrusive for—"

"I'm not worried."

He'd come into the room smiling, happy, and now he seemed upset with her.

"I want you to feel free to do…" He ran a hand through his hair. "To do whatever you like around here."

"All right, I will." A slight pause, and then, "Thank you, Noah."

His blue eyes widened; his jaw dropped. "Don't *thank* me, for goodness' sake." He raised a hand, let it drop against his thigh with a quiet slap. "This is *your* house now, too, you know. You don't need my permission to—"

"You're right. I'm sorry for upsetting you."

He looked at the ceiling, then ran a hand through his hair. "Dara, *please*. Don't *apologize*," he said, meeting her eyes. "I'm not upset, and you haven't done anything to be sorry about."

Coulda fooled me, she thought, pursing her lips.

But she'd promised herself she'd be a patient and understanding wife. Dara did her best to make sense of his attitude. It had been a long, eventful day. He'd eaten a lot of rich food. He'd been forced to sit through that old movie with the kids for the hundredth time. *He woke up a bachelor, and he'll be going to bed a bridegroom.*

"I—I'm...*ouch!*"

"What's wrong?" he asked, genuinely concerned.

She grinned. "I could feel myself starting to apologize again, and I bit my lip...a bit too hard."

"Oh, gee, I'm sorry."

One brow high on her forehead, Dara smiled, then laughed, and so did he.

She tried a different tack. "So...are the kids all tucked in?"

The question coaxed a smile. "Well, they're in bed, but I don't know how ready they are to go to sleep."

She raised her eyebrows, waiting for his explanation.

"Guess they're pretty excited. They weren't expecting a wedding *and* a party."

"Neither was I," she admitted. She bent down, stuffed packing paper into one of the boxes she'd unpacked. "In fact, I've been meaning to ask you. Who planned it?"

His cheeks turned bright red. "Planned what?"

"The wedding."

"W-well, well, *we* did," he stammered, "remember?"

Dara climbed into the box, stamped the papers down with both feet. "No," she said, shaking her head, "what *we* planned was a quickie ceremony in front of Pastor Williams's battered old desk. No witnesses, no music, no—"

"Wasn't my idea," he said, cutting her off. "That stuff…it was in the church when I got there." One shoulder rose as he added, "Guess Williams figured it wouldn't do any harm if we made use of it."

Brow furrowed, she narrowed one eye. "Funny, no one at the reception knew, either."

"Knew what?"

Eyes wide now, she hopped out of the box. "When, where…*that* we were getting married."

He dismissed her comment with a noncommittal shrug. "You know how that kind of news travels."

Yeah, well, she thought, I'm not buying it. Not for a minute. Because the only person Dara had told about the wedding was the principal at Centennial. And he didn't go to their church.

Noah pocketed both hands, leaned forward a bit, stared at the toes of his shoes. "You, ah, you want a cup of tea before we turn in?"

Before we turn in… She liked the comfortable, familiar *married* sound of that.

"I'd love some tea, but only if you'll have a cup, too."

Noah met her eyes, and after a long, penetrating stare, he smiled. "Okay, but only if you'll let me fix it."

She shut the closet door and picked up the cardboard boxes.

"Let me get those," he said, taking them from her.

He started for the door, but her hand on his arm stopped him. "Noah?"

"Hmm?"

"Thanks."

His eyebrows knitted in the center of his forehead. "For what?"

"For whatever strings you pulled," she said, "you know, to make the wedding, the reception…for making it all happen." She tilted her head. "I don't know how you knew it had always been a dream of mine…a wedding like that. It was lovely. Really. So thank you."

For a moment, transfixed by those big brown eyes of hers, Noah couldn't seem to find his voice. Might have been a big mistake, he told himself, trying to give her something better than a "quickie ceremony," because now she'll expect more. Trouble was, he didn't know if he could give her more.

"I didn't do a thing," he said. And it was true; Pastor Williams and his missus had arranged everything.

At Noah's request….

"I'm leaving it in your very capable hands, Williams," he'd insisted as he dashed off a generous check, made payable to the church. "Doesn't need to be fancy. Dara doesn't go for a lot of fuss and bother. But I want her to have flowers, lots of flowers. And friends around her. A nice meal. Some soft drinks and a pretty cake. Someone to take pictures."

"Ah, memories…" the pastor had said, a knowing smile on his face.

"Yeah. Right. Memories." He'd shoved the checkbook back into his jacket pocket. "Whatever's left over after you buy the supplies…belongs to the parish."

It had been worth every dime spent. The good ladies of the congregation had prepared a six-course ham dinner in the little kitchen behind the banquet hall and served it up piping hot on white stoneware. Lucy Barnes had whipped up a beautiful four-layer cake, topped off with the traditional painted-plastic bride and groom. Moe Houghton donated a barrel of root beer. The Kincaid family brought their mandolins and banjos and guitars and created a foot-stompin', hand-clappin' hoedown right there in the church basement. Dara had looked adorable, square dancing in her little white suit and hat.

She'd looked enchanting, laughing and chatting with their friends and neighbors, too. So ravishing, in fact, that he almost forgot how petrified she'd looked earlier.

Almost, but not quite.

She'd stood at the back of the church, wringing her tiny hands in front of her, eyes wide and frightened, like a rabbit caught in the act of enjoying some garden-grown lettuce. He'd wanted to thunder down that white-sheeted aisle and scoop her up in his arms, promise that nothing would ever harm her—not if he could help it!—as long as they both lived.

Which, if God had heard even *one* of the hundreds of prayers he'd said since the day he met her, would be a long, long time.

He glanced at the alarm clock. Eleven-forty.

What's taking her so long? And why is she in there?

They had watched the eleven o'clock news, Dara sprawled on the sofa, sipping the tea he'd brewed her, Noah tilted back in his recliner. Afterward, while he flipped off the lights and locked the doors, she'd gone upstairs. When he rounded the landing, he noticed a pencil-thin streak of light glowing from under the hall bathroom door. Had he said or done anything that had made her feel she wasn't welcome in the master bathroom?

Lying in bed, he stared at the ceiling fan overhead and reflected on their evening.

When they got home after the reception at seven o'clock, Dara had changed into sneakers, leggings and an oversize sweatshirt. When she came downstairs, the first thing he'd noticed was that she'd scrubbed her face clean of eye shadow, lipstick and rouge. How could she be pushin' thirty? he'd wondered as she'd bustled around the kitchen, preparing a snack from the party leftovers the church ladies had packed up, when she barely looks twenty-one!

They'd had a grand time, he and the kids and Dara, sitting around the table, recalling the events of the day as they nibbled at ham sandwiches and potato salad, baked beans and coleslaw. He couldn't remember the last time the kids had been so happy, so animated.

Yes, he could.

Every time they're around her, he'd told himself.

After supper, she'd excused herself to finish unpacking while he and the kids watched an old movie for the hundredth time. Then he'd tucked the kids into bed and listened to their prayers and joined her in the bedroom—correction, their bedroom—where he found her on her hands and knees in the closet. They'd had a short but friendly conversation, and he'd carried her empty packing boxes downstairs, and while she said good-night to the kids, he'd brewed them both a cup of tea.

Nothing that would make her feel unwelcome, he told himself.

Then they'd watched the last half of a show about a cat and a newspaperman or something, and the news. Anyway, he thought that's what they'd watched; Noah hadn't really been paying much attention to the TV.

Because he couldn't keep his eyes off Dara.

In the trim-fitting pants and baggy sweatshirt, she'd reminded him of a fresh-faced teenage girl, stretched out on the couch with a bowl of popcorn in her lap and a mug of tea at her side. During a commercial in the cat program, she'd gotten up to make them another cup of tea, and when she'd leaned across him to get his mug, Noah got a whiff of her perfume. Like lilacs in the springtime, he'd thought, and it had been all he could do to keep from pulling her into his lap and smothering her with kisses.

For that next half hour, as the local news anchor read reports about the state police crackdown on aggressive drivers and the joke-cracking meteorologist delivered another forecast for snow, Noah had wondered what on earth the two of them were doing on a Saturday night, watching TV in his family room. They should have been walking hand in hand on a deserted beach on some exotic island in the Caribbean. This is your wedding night, after all, he'd thought.

Covering his face with the pillow, Noah shook his head. You're a numbers man, he told himself. You don't let things slip through the cracks.

But the truth was, he hadn't *forgotten* about the honeymoon. Quite the contrary. He'd been *afraid* to plan one, because what if he did—she'd go along with it, of course, because that's the way she was—but what if he planned a romantic getaway and Dara gave some slight hint that she didn't *want* to be alone with him? She'd married him to clear her father's name, to see that his kids were properly cared for. And a honeymoon, well, that was for people in *love*.

Wasn't it?

Okay, so the big question now was, would she want

to consummate their vows…ever…or did she view this a marriage in name only?

You could ask her, he thought, if she'd ever come out of the bathroom!

But he wouldn't ask her, and he knew it.

Because he was as afraid of that answer as he'd been of the honeymoon.

He tucked the pillow under his head again, linked his fingers together under it. Everything just happened too fast was the answer he immediately gave himself.

But it was a poor excuse, and a lie to boot. Because the truth of the matter was, he'd fallen feet over forehead for Dara, almost from the moment she'd walked into her father's office at Pinnacle Construction wearing that neat blue teacher's suit, shiny curls bouncing, bright brown eyes flashing, smiling.

Even if he'd been uncertain then, he'd known it a week or so later, when she'd come to dinner at Bobby's invitation. He'd taken her in his arms not once but twice! He remembered thinking at the time of a Top-40 song, recorded during the seventies, that went something like "love fits like a hand in a glove." That was how Dara felt in his arms…as if she'd been created just for him by the Almighty Himself.

"Which switch turns out the lamp?" she asked, interrupting his thoughts.

Noah cleared his throat and lifted his head in time to see her pointing at the double switch plate on the wall near the bedroom door. Now, really; how did she expect him to think straight when she looked like *that?*

She wore a floor-length white cotton nightgown with soft ruffles at the sleeves and hem. He'd never seen her bare feet before, but they were just as slender and shapely as the rest of her. It surprised him—that little bit of shocking red on her toenails—but it was a delightful surprise. You're a vision, he thought, swallowing. You look like a princess in that getup.

Impatience must have gotten the best of her, because Dara flipped the switch nearest the door—and started the ceiling fan to spinning above him. "Uh, that one turns on the, ah—"

"The ceiling fan?" she finished, smiling.

He nodded.

"And this one?" She flipped it, turning on the light fixture attached to the fan. Turning off the fan and the overhead light, she said, "Looks like you're in charge of lights out."

It seemed to Noah that she floated, rather than walked, toward the bed, the flowing, billowing nightdress trailing behind her like...

Like the train of a wedding gown.

His heart beat like a parade drum, his pulse and breathing accelerating as she pulled back the covers and slipped between the sheets.

"Okay," she said, rolling onto her side to face him, "I'm ready."

Ready?

His heart was pounding now, knocking against his ribs, battering his spine. He wondered if she could feel it, like tiny hammer blows, thudding against the mattress.

Ready? Ready for what?

And then it dawned on him in a quick and disappointing moment...all that talk about which switch worked which light. Levering himself up on one elbow, he rolled to his right, nearly knocking the alarm from the nightstand as he reached for the lamp. Gritting his teeth, he twisted its knob and doused the room in blackness. "You want me to turn the bathroom light on?" he whispered.

"Whatever for?" she whispered back.

"In case you need to—"

"I'll be fine."

He could tell by the sound of her voice that she was still facing him.

"In a few minutes," she continued, "my eyes will get used to the dark. I eat a lot of carrots. Good for night vision, you know," she nervously chattered.

Chuckling, Noah shook his head. "I don't know about carrots, but sometimes, you're a nut."

She sang that part of a popular candy bar commercial.

Rolling onto his left side to face her, he said, "And sometimes you're not."

Dara crooned the rest of the jingle.

Without thinking, Noah reached out, rested a hand on her shoulder. When he realized what he'd done, he half expected her to draw away, to stiffen with fright, to gasp. But she did none of those things. Instead, Dara gave his fingertips a light pat-pat-pat and a gentle squeeze.

And she didn't let go.

Could it mean what he hoped it meant?

Or was it nothing more than a friendly gesture? You'll never know if you don't—

"Noah?"

"Hmm."

"Why do you suppose that, when the lights go out, people tend to whisper?"

Smiling, he shrugged. "Guess the darkness is a signal of some sort, telling people to be calm, to be quiet, the way nature stills and silences the earth."

"Aha...."

"'Aha' what?"

"I've married a poet, I see."

He scooted closer, slowly slid his hand from her shoulder to her upper back and, laughing softly, said, "You mean like 'How do I love thee? Let me count the ways'?"

A moment of complete quiet went by. "Something like that."

He wished he could see her face so he'd know what that slight change in her musical voice meant. He moved closer still, wrapped both arms around her, again prepared for her to stiffen, to hold him at arm's length, to turn away.

Again she didn't.

Snuggling her face into the crook of his neck, Dara exhaled a long, slow sigh. And the sound of it wrapped around him like a warm blanket. Eyes closed, he kissed her forehead. "I hope I didn't hurt your feelings earlier."

"Hmm?"

"When you were talking about your wolf collection, and I said—"

"You didn't."

He felt her shrug.

"I just figured you were feeling guilty," she said, "for breaking your promise. That you didn't quite know what to make of having another woman in your house."

"What promise?"

"You said once that she asked you to promise that you'd find the kids a mother substitute as soon as possible. You said you told her what she needed to hear, but that you'd promised yourself no one would ever take her place.''

If you told Dara that, he thought, *you're an insensitive jerk.*

"Francine was never in this house. She never set foot in this room," he said. "She died nearly three years before we moved to the Baltimore area, remember?"

She nodded.

"And just to set the record straight, I sold every stick of furniture when I put the Pennsylvania property on the market."

She leaned back a bit. "You did?"

He nodded.

"But why? Weren't there...weren't there memories attached to those things?"

Noah sighed heavily. "That's exactly why I left them behind."

"Oh," she said in a very small voice.

"Hasn't been easy, has it?"

"What hasn't?"

"Everything. You don't even have an engagement ring."

He felt her wrap her left hand in her right. "This little band of gold is all I'll ever need, Noah."

She was different, all right.

"But you had to endure a throw-together marriage service and a hasty reception, and—"

"I loved the ceremony, and the reception, too." She shook her shoulders. "In fact, I can hardly wait until the pictures are developed."

"Yeah, well... Then you're forced to sleep in here, with me, so the kids won't think—"

"It hasn't exactly been a picnic for you, either."
Almost immediately, Dara began to laugh.

He shook his head. "What's so funny?"

"Have you ever planned a picnic?"

Noah swallowed the urge to say, What does *that*
have to do with anything? "Can't say as I have," he
said, instead.

"It's not so easy, you know, remembering everything—tablecloth and napkins, plates and silverware,
something to drink and something to drink from, something to keep hot food hot and cold food cold and—"

He thought maybe he was beginning to understand
her...a little. "I get it."

He heard the smile in her voice when she nodded.

They seemed content, after that, to lie quietly in each
other's arms. Listening to her soft, steady breaths was
as comforting as the gentle sound of rain on the roof,
and Noah was lulled into a near sleep state. It felt so
good, holding her this way, that he had no idea how
much time had passed since he'd turned out the light.

After a while, her sleepy voice broke the silence.
"Noah?"

"Hmm."

"We, um. We never discussed the...the details."

"What details?" he mumbled groggily.

Sleepy or not, he had to consider the possibility that
maybe he understood her a little *too* well, for he
thought he knew what she was referring to. But much
as he longed for her, Noah would not risk frightening
her or making her feel put-upon. Because he couldn't
forget what Dara had said: "My father gets his good
name back. You'll get chief cook and bottle washer,
and your kids get a substitute mother. What's in it for
me?"

His eyes had grown accustomed to the darkness by now, and in the narrow shaft of light that squeaked under the window shade, he could see her beautiful, wide-eyed face. Oh, how he longed for even one kiss from his wife. Noah swallowed hard. Took a deep breath. But the time wasn't right. She had to trust him first, to know how much he cared for her. "We have the rest of our lives," he whispered, "to work out the details."

Her cheek pressed to his chest, she murmured something.

"What's that, sweetie?" he asked without even thinking, running his fingers through her hair.

"I know it's been a busy, hectic day," she said, stifling a yawn, "but I was just wondering…"

"Wondering what?"

"What were you thinking, standing up there on the altar, when Pastor Williams said 'Do you take this woman…'"

Noah looked into her eyes, which seemed bigger, browner, downright fathomless, in the nearly dark room. Should he tell her the truth? That he was thinking, Get on with it, so I can seal this deal with a kiss! Should he admit that his palms had started sweating and his heart had started thumping as though he'd just run a marathon?

Should he tell her that it had taken every ounce of his control to keep from blurting out that he loved her, that he felt like the luckiest man on earth knowing she'd consented to marry him…for whatever reasons?

No. The truth would only put pressure on her, and that was the last thing he wanted to do.

One hand on either side of her face, he repeated her

question. "What do you mean, 'What was I thinking?'"

Her eyes sparkled like coal in the moonlight as she gazed into his face. "I mean, was there a moment when you asked yourself, 'Is this a mistake?' Was there a point when you considered ducking out the door and—"

He pressed a fingertip to her lips, silencing her. "No," he said sincerely, "nothing like that went through my head, not even for an instant."

A smile gentled her features. "But how could you be so sure?"

"Because," he began, "I've never done anything without first consulting God. At least, not since Angie and Bobby came along."

Dara nodded. "I see."

Was that…was that sadness in her voice? "What about you?" he asked. "Did you have any second thoughts at the last minute?"

"No," she said, "not really."

The words had been what he'd wanted to hear, but she'd said them a beat too late, and she'd stiffened slightly when she'd said them, which could only mean one thing: she *had* given a thought or two to calling the wedding off. The realization awakened an ache in him like none he'd known to date.

"Remember when I asked you, selfishly, what was in it for me?"

"I remember." He doubted he'd ever forget. "But the question wasn't the least bit selfish. You had every right to be concerned about your future."

His response seemed to calm her, and she relaxed again in his arms. "I think I know what's in it for me now."

His heart soared with hopefulness. "What's in it for you, Dara?" he husked.

She nestled closer still. "I love Angie and Bobby—"

"I know that," he interrupted. "Anyone with eyes knows that."

"But," she continued, "what's in it for me…is a baby."

Was he hearing things? Had she really said—

"I've been praying about it ever since you first popped the question," Dara said. "There's so much love in this house. I think we'd have a lot to offer a baby. A baby would be good for the kids, would be good for us all." She sighed sweetly. "I've wanted a child of my own for as long as I can remember. I hate to use a cliché, but my biological clock is ticking even louder than that old-fashioned alarm of yours." Smiling, she tilted her head back, stared into his eyes. "*That's* what's in it for me, Noah."

"A baby…."

She nodded again.

He was about to tell her he'd never deny her anything, especially not something as miraculous, as magnificent as a baby, when she pressed her lips to his.

Chapter Ten

Instinct made him slide his hand around to her nape to draw her nearer still, and this time when their lips met, he tried to tell her with his kiss how he felt, how much he'd like to give her...how his heart was overflowing with love for her...feelings he could never describe with words alone....

Gently, lovingly, he ended their kiss and pressed his fingertips to her lips. "A baby, huh?"

"Yes," she said, nodding, "a baby."

A shudder went through him as he looked into her long-lashed, closed eyes. "You're beautiful," he whispered, "so beautiful...."

Slowly, her lids opened, and dreamily, she looked at him, and went completely still. "So are you."

His forefinger traced the curve of her jaw, the slope of her throat. He loved her with all his heart and soul. They'd have children together. Face life's ups and downs together. Grow old together.

Together.

The word was like a rainbow after a thunderstorm.

Her eyes glittered with unshed tears as he kissed her. She twined her arms around his neck, drove her fingers through his hair and sighed, a long, melodious sound that reminded him of the wind chimes Brother Constantine had hung in the garden at St. Vincent's.

"I think you should know something first."

He felt her stiffen, shift a bit, as if preparing to pull away.

"I—I'm…" She sighed and, exasperated, winnowed her fingers through her hair. "I don't want to disappoint you, that's all."

"Disappoint me?"

"It's… I'm not very…experienced."

He chuckled humorlessly. "How experienced are you?"

Dara heaved a loud sigh. "The truth of it is, you've married yourself a thirty-year-old virgin."

It stunned him a bit, the way she'd said it, as though she expected he'd be ashamed of her *in*experience. "First of all, I thought your birthday was in May."

"It is."

"Then I've married myself a twenty-nine-year-old virgin."

Dara smiled. "I stand corrected."

He kissed the tip of her nose. "Second, why do you say it as though you're ashamed, as though it's something disgraceful? I think it's wonderful."

"I'm not ashamed. I know a lot of people these days think that for a woman to save herself for her husband is an old-fashioned notion. But I believe it's the right thing to do."

He nodded. "I agree."

She shook her head. "I don't think it's the least bit

disgraceful. Discouraging, maybe…a little unsatisfying, even.''

"For me, you mean?"

Burrowing her face deeper into his shoulder, she nodded.

"Sweetie," he said, "look at me."

When she didn't, he cupped her chin in his palm, lifted her face until their eyes met. "You could never disappoint me."

Her face broke into a smile so bright it could have lit the room, and when she kissed him, a muted sigh escaped her lips. He felt as if he might drown in the lazy pleasure of it.

Until the unhappy fact dawned.

Somewhere, way off in the deepest recesses of his subconscious, he acknowledged that as much as he'd hoped and prayed for this, Dara didn't want their marriage to be a true one because she loved him. She'd said it in her usual kindhearted way, of course, but she'd made it clear nonetheless: he was the necessary means by which her dream of motherhood would become a reality.

He was a trained auditor and could easily add things up.

He held her gently in the curve of his arm, gazed longingly at her. She'd done so much for him, for Bobby and Angie, and he had a feeling she hadn't even begun to make a home for them yet. If a baby would fulfill a wish, answer a prayer, make a dream come true, then she should have one…or a dozen babies, if that was what she wanted! Having grown up an orphan, he had more cause than most to consider each child a gift from God, would love and treasure every one she'd give him with every beat of his heart.

God had better have mercy on his miserable soul and provide him with strength—a double dose of it—in case this marriage of convenience he'd set up turned out to be just that...and nothing more.

Dara awoke to the sound of a phone trilling somewhere off in the distance. Rolling onto her back, she yawned and stretched, squinted into the bright sunshine peeking around the edges of the window shade. She must have imagined the telephone's ring. Either that or one of the kids had—

The kids....

With a flush of sudden warmth, Dara remembered where she was. Remembered *who* she was now...and that last night, she'd become Mrs. Noah Lucas in every sense of the word.

She had lain awake for hours afterward, thinking about the splendor of it all. If the man-woman union could be so nearly perfect when only one or the other was in love, Dara could only imagine how much more a couple might expect when the devotion, the desire, the love, flowed both ways.

It had been a risk, telling him what she expected to gain from this marriage. She had considered the possibility that Noah might not want to consummate their marriage, that two children were all he could handle, that he had no intention—or desire—to replace Francine, in *any* way. But, like the answer to a prayer, Noah had seemed almost pleased by her announcement. Not so surprising, really, when she considered his childhood, when she thought of how hard he tried to be a good father to Angie and Bobby.

On her side now, she scrunched the pillow under her neck so she could watch her new husband sleep. He lay on his back, right hand resting lightly on his chest, left hand flat on the mattress, just inches from her thigh.

Last night, those hands had touched her with such tenderness, as if he believed she were made of delicate crystal and one wrong move might shatter her.

His hair poked out in all directions, making her want to reach out and smooth it into place, the way she had in the darkness, when a lock of burnished blond fell across one eye, blocking his vision.

Long, thick lashes beneath the smooth brow dusted rugged cheekbones, and his slightly parted mustached mouth emitted a soft whistle with each exhalation. The slight smile that curved his beautiful lips up at the corners told her that his dreams, like his face, were at peace. *Are you dreaming of Francine?* she wondered, linking her fingers with his.

It was foolish—no, *dangerous*—to ask such questions, because the answers were torture, pure torture. And yet, the fact that he still cared for his departed wife made him all the more lovable. Because if he could feel so strongly about a woman he'd lost over three years ago how much more could he love her, if only he'd give himself a chance!

The children thundered up the stairs, making her wonder where the old expression, "pitter-patter of little feet" had come from. Two little fists knocked on the door.

"Father," Angie called, "it's Grandmother!"

Opening one eye, he wrinkled his nose. "Wha…?"

Dara tossed back the covers and shrugged into her robe. "It's your mother-in-law," she whispered, hugging the collar tight to her throat. "She's on the phone."

"My mother-in-*what*?"

Dara tied the robe's belt. "Your—"

"Father? Are you awake?"

Gently, Dara shook his shoulder. "Noah... Noah, wake up! It's Francine's mother," she said, a little more loudly this time.

He pulled the pillow over his face. "What time is it?" came his muffled question.

"Nearly nine." She ran around to the other side of the bed and tugged at his covers.

The knocking increased in volume and intensity. "Fa-ther!"

"Noah, please. The children are right outside, no doubt with the portable phone in their—"

He hugged the comforter tighter and groaned. "What does she want?" he moaned, crooking an arm over his eyes.

"There's only one way to find out." Dara flung the quilt back, exposing long hairy legs that poked out from blue-striped boxer shorts, muscles that bulged under the snug sleeves of his white T-shirt.

After one last attempt to hold on to the disappearing blanket, he sat up. Planting both feet on the carpet, he shook his head. "C'mon in, kids," he invited.

The door flew open as if it had been spring loaded, and Angie and Bobby burst into the room. Jumping onto the bed, they bounced around near him, giggling as they hugged him, kissed him, tousled his already mussed hair.

Angie held out the phone. "Grandmother says there hasn't been any snow at all in Florida. She says she misses the change of seasons. She says she misses us, too, and that she wants to come and see us."

Closing his eyes, Noah hung his head. "Lord, give me strength," he whispered.

"What did you say, Father?"

Tucking in one corner of his mouth, he accepted the phone from his daughter. "Emmaline!" he said, standing. "How are you?"

Dara watched as he nodded and frowned, nodded and smiled, nodded and shook his head. After a while, Noah said, "That'll be fine, Emmaline, just fine." Another minute of silence passed as he raised his eyebrows, pinched the bridge of his nose with thumb and forefinger, drove his fingers through his hair. "That's right, Emmaline, yesterday. Yes, yes. I'm sorry you couldn't make it, too."

Then, "Aha, aha...." He sat on the edge of the bed, shoulders slumped.

"Mmm-hmm. Is that right?" He leaned forward, hid his face behind his free hand.

"Sure, sure...." More silence, more nodding.

"I'm sure she won't." He sighed and listened.

"Yes, we're happy." He met Dara's eyes for a moment and smiled slightly. "Very happy." Then he closed his eyes and clenched his teeth.

"Of course not. She'd never do—"

He stood. Frowned. "Not in a million years! She's nothing like that, Emmaline." More nodding, another shake of the head.

"That's right, you'll see for yourself. All right, then, we'll wait to hear from you. Aha. Mmm-hmm. Okay. We love you, too. Bye...."

He depressed the phone's off button, handed the phone back to Angie. "Thanks, honey," he said, scratching his whiskered chin. "Did you guys have breakfast?"

"We had Fruity Oats," Bobby volunteered.

"And orange juice," Angie added.

He ruffled their hair. "Good. Let's get cleaned up now, or we'll be late for church. Services start in just over an hour, you know."

"May I wear my wedding dress?" Angie wanted to know.

"I don't see why not."

"Can I wear jeans and sneakers?"

"*May* I," Angie corrected.

He sighed and, narrowing his eyes, said, "So *can* I...*Dad?*"

Noah's brows rose high on his forehead in response to the moniker. "What makes you think you could get away with that?"

"Well," he started, grinning, "I'm still re-re-*recuperating....*"

"Recuperating?" Noah echoed, grinning back. "Your vocabulary has improved since your last spelling test, you little con man. You'll wear your suit. As usual."

Dara had been standing off to the side, quietly taking it all in. She took half a step forward and stuffed her hands into the pockets of her robe. "So when is...Grandmother arriving?" she ventured.

His mustache tilted in a half grin and his blue eyes lit up with mischief. "Well, it's like this, li'l missy. Grandmaw will be rollin' in on the eight-oh-four," he drawled, walking around the room like an old, bow-legged cowboy. "We-uns will need t' be down at the station a tick or two afore that, though, just in case the ole chuggaroo pulls in a mite early."

Giggling, Angie hugged Noah around the waist. "Oh, Father," she said. "You're funny!"

But Dara failed to see the humor in his words.

"How long…" Dara cleared her throat. "Will she be staying with us long?"

"Ay-yup," Bobby said, continuing his father's geezer imitation. "She'll be stowin' her gear in the ole spare bedroom right on through the holidays."

Eyes widening, Dara clutched at her throat. "Through…" She swallowed hard. "Until…until *after Christmas?*"

"Until January third," Angie offered. "She wants to help us ring in the New Year."

Let me get this straight, Dara told herself. My new husband's deceased wife's mother is coming to town, tonight, and she's staying… Dara did some quick mental calculating. She's staying two weeks!

"Grandfather is coming, too," Bobby said, nodding excitedly. "He's attired."

Angie's shoulders slumped with frustration. "*Re*-tired," she said. And facing Dara, she added, "That means he doesn't have to go to work anymore."

"'Cause he's old."

"Not old," his sister scolded. She looked to her father for guidance. "He's just…"

Smiling, Noah raised a brow. "He's your grampa. That's all you need to know."

Dara could almost hear her father asking, Do you love your mother? Then what else matters?

Noah bent down, gave each child a kiss on the cheek, then patted their round little bottoms. "Go on, now," he said, leading them to the door. "Start getting ready, and maybe we can avoid our usual Sunday rush."

"Yes, Father." Angie skipped through the doorway and quickly disappeared down the hall.

"Sho' 'nuff, Pa," Bobby said. "You want I should wear me a bow tie aroun' mah neck?"

"Pardner," Noah replied, squinting one eye, "y'all decide that for yo'seff. Now, listen to yer pa and mosey along."

Snickering, Bobby hop-skipped from the room. "I ain't a-gonna wear no bow tie!" he hollered over his shoulder. "Just try an' make me!"

Noah stood in the middle of the room for a moment, grinning and shaking his head. Then, turning to Dara, he said, "You're sure you want another one of those running around here?"

"You bet I am." What I don't want around here, she added mentally, are Francine's parents!

Noah crossed the room in three long strides and rested his hands on her shoulders. "Don't worry," he said softly. "They don't bite."

She couldn't make herself meet his eyes. "It's just that... Two weeks is such a long time, Noah. A *very* long time." She bit her lower lip to still its trembling. Everything was happening too fast. *Way* too fast. She'd only just met Noah and the children six weeks earlier and now—

A terrible thought pinged in her mind: what if Francine's parents jumped to the conclusion that she and Noah had been in a rush to get married because they were in trouble?

Running both hands through her hair, she expelled a long, shuddering sigh.

"Sweetie," Noah said, a fingertip lifting her chin, "look at me."

When she did, he pressed a light kiss to her forehead. "They're..." He paused, as if groping for words. "You'll..." His smile was forced. "You'll like them."

Oh, really? she asked silently. Then why do you look as though the hangman just slipped a noose around your neck?

"I'll be right here." He pulled her close and kissed the top of her head. "I promised I'd take care of you, and I will." Releasing her, he headed for the door. "I think I'll have a cup of coffee while you get ready for church."

"Okay."

"Want me to bring you a cup?"

"Sure." She smiled shakily. "That'd be nice."

He started down the stairs, then ran back into the room. "Dara?"

She was halfway to the bathroom by now. "Hmm?"

"Wear that red velvet thing-y." He wiggled his eyebrows. "Brings out the bloom in your cheeks."

Her smile grew; her heart fluttered. How could she refuse him such a small request? Get real, Dara, she thought. You couldn't refuse him anything.

"All right…if you'll wear your blue sweater." She winked. "Brings out the blue of your eyes."

"Deal," he said. And then he was gone.

A glance at the clock told Dara she had just about ten hours to get ready for her unexpected, extended guests. Well, she told herself, adjusting the water temperature for her shower, life around here is going to be a lot of things, but boring isn't one of them!

Francine alphabetized her spice rack.

Francine ironed the bedsheets.

Francine scrubbed the bathroom tile after every shower.

Francine grew prizewinning roses.

Dara had heard enough Francine accolades to last

her a lifetime, though Emmaline and Joseph had been in town only three days. But this last one, well, it was all she could do to hold her tongue.

"You've outdone yourself tonight, Dara," Emmaline gushed, dabbing a napkin to the corners of her lipsticked mouth. "Even better than last night."

Anyone with eyes could see that the woman didn't approve of the meal, for it was written all over her narrow, pinched face. "Thank you, Emmaline," Dara said stiffly.

Last night, Dara had whipped up a pot of Irish stew. Noah's former mother-in-law took one bite and, clucking her tongue, said, "Mmm...different." After which Emmaline pointed out that Francine's stew contained sage.

The evening before, when Francine's parents had arrived, she'd cooked up her specialty...stuffed shells. And what had Emmaline said?

"They're quite tasty...."

"I know that tone," her husband had said. And with a wry smile, he'd added, "We won't get a moment's peace until she's finished." Grasping his wife's hand, Joseph smiled. "Tell us, Emmaline."

"Why, Joseph," she'd sputtered, "whatever do you mean?"

"'They're quite tasty,'" he said, doing an almost perfect imitation of her. "I distinctly heard a 'but' at the end of that sentence. Out with it, dear. 'They're quite tasty...'" He waved an encouraging hand in the air. "'Bu-u-u-ut....'"

Pursing her lips, she'd lifted her double chins, expelled a feigned maternal sigh. "You didn't use fresh basil, did you, Dara dear?" She looked at Noah. "Francine always used fresh basil in her tomato sauce."

She'd given his hand a squeeze. "She was such a wonderful cook, wasn't she, darling?"

Wearing a strained smile, he'd said, "Yes. Wonderful."

And now, as if to add insult to injury, Emmaline was crinkling her upturned little nose at Dara's pot roast. "Noah, darling," she said, "you saved Francine's recipe box, didn't you?"

"It's in the pantry," Angie offered.

"Thank you, darling," she gushed, smiling at her granddaughter.

Then, aiming a thin-lipped grin in Dara's direction, she added, "Perhaps Noah will let you have a look at it." This time it was Dara's hand that she squeezed. "I'm sure your heart is in the right place...that your intentions for Noah and the children are only the best, dear." She tilted her head, as if to say, But you're falling far short of the mark...*dear.*

"A new bride can use all the help she can get, after all."

Lord, Dara prayed, gritting her teeth, *give me strength or I'll—*

"Especially while she's learning to become a good wife...."

Dara had pulled out the battered old etiquette book her great-grandmother had brought over from England, so the table settings would be correct. And she'd pressed the damask tablecloth and matching napkins her mother had cherished. There hadn't been a speck, not a single water spot, on the china or the crystal. And the silver had been polished to perfection.

While the rest of them slept, she'd scurried around the darkened, silent house, scrubbing, dusting, buffing—hoping and praying, as she straightened books on the shelves and fluffed pillows on the sofas, that she might come close, at least, to measuring up to Francine...

Who'd ironed Noah's socks and alphabetized the pantry and mowed the lawn...with a toenail clipper, no doubt!

But try as she might, she hadn't measured up. Hadn't even come close, to hear Emmaline tell it.

And it wasn't likely that she ever would.

Slowly, deliberately, Dara scooted her chair back from the table. Standing, she began stacking dishes, salad bowls, bread plates.

"Heavens," Emmaline said, "I haven't offended you, have I, dear?"

Dara lifted a column of plates and, forcing a smile, said in cautious, even tones, "The Lord blessed me with the hide of a rhinoceros, Mrs. Brewster. There's very little that can offend me."

She didn't wait for a response. Instead, Dara headed straight for the kitchen, where she deposited the dishes on the counter with a clatter. Then she trudged to the table, slumped into a chair and held her head in her hands. *I don't ask for much, Lord,* Dara prayed, *just a little peace and quiet in this crazy life. I didn't complain—did I?—when Mom got sick. You heard no whimpering from me when Dad had his first heart attack...even though You knew how afraid I was of losing him...of being all alone.*

And when he died, she didn't whine. She had accepted his death and continued to do His will. Even when she'd learned of the embezzlement, Dara hadn't questioned God. Despite the humiliation, the anger, the pain, she had not doubted the Lord.

Her ego had never been put to such a test before,

and Emmaline, she feared, was more than she could handle. No, make that Francine....

She thought she could handle knowing that Noah still cared so deeply for the woman. Thought she could deal with his quiet devotion, his missing her, his tribute to her memory. Because he had agreed, on their wedding night, to give her what she'd wanted more than anything in this world: a child. A child of her own! And that, she believed, would more than make up for the fact that she'd committed her future to a man who was in love with his former wife.

But she'd been wrong. So very wrong. *I don't know if I have what it takes, Sweet Jesus, to live in Francine's shadow.*

What *did* they all want from her, anyway? Wasn't it enough that she loved and cared for Angie and Bobby as if they were her own? And which was really better for them: no-nonsense discipline and a flawlessly spotless house, or a mother who loved them simply because they'd been born? Dara would never subject the kids to the disorganization and disruption of the topsy-turvy household she'd grown up in, but she refused to become the drill sergeant Francine had been, either! If that's what they want, they're in for a rude awakening, she thought, sniffing, because—

"Dara?"

Did he really think that nothing more than the weight of his hand on her shoulder would restore her, reassure her? She didn't want his support now; she'd needed it at the table, while Emmaline had been ridiculing her cooking, her housekeeping skills, her laid-back "let them be children" mind-set.

"If I'd known it would be like this," he said, "I never would have—"

She wiped her eyes on the backs of her hands. "Where is she?" Dara asked without turning.

"Upstairs. With Joseph and the kids." He paused, rested both hands on her shoulders.

Joseph, Dara scoffed. Why not "Joe"? Who's Emmaline trying to impress with this uppity nonsense? Noah had told Dara all about Emmaline's background, about how she'd risen, like the phoenix, from her impoverished childhood, to become one of Baltimore's rich and famous. But it hadn't been by dint of hard work that she'd achieved her lofty status; her marriage to Joseph—whose family's business had been a Maryland institution for nearly two centuries—had been the means by which she'd had access to Boca Raton real estate, a sprawling ranch in horse country, luxury vehicles and partying with the state's most illustrious political and corporate leaders. God doesn't love her any more or any less than He loves any of His children, Dara fumed, so where does she get off putting me down just because—

"Dara, look at me."

She'd put out four place mats and cloth napkins after services on Sunday, then chose her biggest, healthiest African violet as a centerpiece, so that when Francine's parents arrived, she could invite them into the kitchen for tea and cookies, make them feel warm and welcome and *at home*.

Ironic, she thought dismally, but it worked so well that Emmaline feels it's well within her rights to belittle me in front of Noah, and Angie, and Bobby.

Sometime during her pity fest, she must have mussed a napkin. Standing, Dara straightened it. "I guess I'd better get the dishes from the dining room. Mashed potatoes set up like concrete if you don't rinse them before—''

''I said look at me.''

If I do, she told him silently, I'll lose control.

And that, she believed, was the biggest mistake she could make right now. For better, for worse, she had vowed. Did you mean it? she asked herself.

The answer, of course, was yes.

Then you'd better find the strength to live in Francine's shadow, because it's painfully obvious that that's where you're going to spend the rest of your life!

Dara took a shaky breath and squared her shoulders.

He turned her to face him. ''You're my wife. I don't like the way she's treating you.'' If she had read insincerity in those sea blue eyes, things would have been different. But he'd meant every word, and his simple, straightforward honesty shattered the last of her composure. His brawny arms slid around her, supporting, consoling, uplifting.

She'd always had plenty of pity for others, when tears crumpled their reserve; for herself, though, weeping seemed pointless and self-centered. Far better—and more productive—to spend that energy seeking out ways to solve whatever problem had brought on the self-pity in the first place!

But standing in the protective circle of his arms, clinging like a needy child, felt strangely fitting and proper, because her weakness had enabled her to draw from his strength.

''I've made up my mind. She's out of here. They're going to be leaving early, because I won't allow *anyone* to talk to my wife that way. I'm so sorry for putting you through this.''

The slight hitch in his voice made her ache. How

self-centered of her, how narrow-minded, not to have seen it before: the Brewsters were the only family Noah had ever known. For better or for worse, she reminded herself. She had the love of his sweet children, for the "better," and Francine's parents for the "worse."

"No," she said, "*I'm* sorry."

He frowned. "For what?"

She sighed. "For behaving like a spoiled little brat. You can't make them leave, the kids would be so disappointed. They're the only grandparents Angie and Bobby will ever have. Besides, I can't blame Emmaline...she misses Francine, and I imagine I pose quite a threat to her, being the woman to take her daughter's place and all." She tidied his shirt collar, brushed a speck of lint from his shoulder. "I'll be more understanding from now on. The rest of their visit will be fun-filled and spectacular. I'll see to it. I promise!"

She didn't know how much time passed as he stood there, studying her face, but if it had been in her power, Dara would have stopped every clock in the world indefinitely. Because for those few moments, as he held her close and looked deep into her eyes, it felt an awful lot as if he loved her.

"You're a piece of work," he said, smiling.

Raising one eyebrow, she smiled back. "I'm not sure I know how to take that."

"Take it to mean there's not another one like you, not anywhere in the universe."

"Which is probably a good thing, and before you try and argue with that, too," she said, a hand up to forestall his reply, "may I remind you the mashed potatoes are turning to cement as we speak?"

Noah chuckled. "All right. Get your riveter out if it'll make you feel any better."

Actually, standing here like this for the rest of her life was what would make her feel better.

But Emmaline was sure to have a barbed commentary about that, and Dara had only just given her word to try to be more understanding of the woman's feelings. "Thank you," she said as she started for the dining room.

"For what?"

Hard as it was, Dara tore her gaze from his and shook her head. "For being you."

She said a little prayer that he wouldn't follow her, and thankfully, God answered it. It was as she stood at the sink, wrist deep in warm foamy dishwater that Dara's memories gripped her....

For a moment there, the other night as they'd clung to each other in the wide, white-sheeted bed, she'd felt a bit sinful for having expressed her wish to have his children, despite the fact that he hadn't fully committed to her. His eyes had blazed in the dim light when he'd said, "A baby?"

He'd wanted a baby, too. She had sensed it so strongly it was as though God had sent an angel to sigh it into her ear. And the knowledge warmed her like August sunshine.

Gently, oh so gently, he'd combed his fingers through her hair. "You're so beautiful," he'd whispered. And then his mouth had covered hers with an insistent, yet achingly tender kiss that touched Dara's very soul. She loved him, wholly and completely, and wanted to prove it with everything that she had, with everything that she was.

And he had been pleased. She could see the happiness and surprise in his eyes, but there had been something else. Tenderness? Affection? Dare she hope for love? Say it, she'd willed him, tell me that you love me!

Sadly, he hadn't said anything. The only sound had been the quiet hiss of the quilt sliding to the floor. That, and the ever-present *click* of the alarm clock, counting off the minutes.

In the quiet moments afterward, she'd snuggled contentedly against him, thrilled at the love she felt for him. She'd fought the feeling long enough; giving in to it at last had been a blessed, comforting relief. It'll be good for the kids, she'd thought drowsily, good for Noah, good for the babies we'll have....

Head high, she scrubbed the last stubborn stain from the roasting pan. To her surprise and relief, they'd left her alone with her womanly chores...and her womanly thoughts.

He was a good and decent man. Proud and determined, Dara believed he would keep his promise to take good care of her always. And she'd keep her oath to him to do the same. It might never be a rockets-and-heartthrobs kind of marriage, she told herself, but it'll be rock solid and long-lasting. She knew that the way she knew her name was now Dara *Lucas,* legally, spiritually, physically....

So much had been said—without words—that night. But her heart ached with a bittersweet yearning for what *hadn't* been said. *Let him love me,* was her sad, silent prayer. *Please, God, let him love me!*

Chapter Eleven

Emmaline had insisted on "helping" with the decorations...and the baking and the shopping and the gift wrapping....

And since Dara was determined to make this Christmas as perfect as it could possibly be, for the children *and* for Noah, she hadn't fought Francine's mother for control.

It turned out to be a blessing, actually, because while Emmaline ran around town, trying desperately to pull things together for the commercial side of the holiday, Dara enjoyed the season for its spiritual aspects.

She'd taken long walks with the kids down the snow-covered neighborhood sidewalks, sat between them on the family room sofa, reading fairy tales— Bobby's favorite story, the "Three Pigs"; Angie's, "Little Red Riding Hood." She'd read the yarns so often, Dara believed she could recite them word for word from the *Big Book of Fables*.

And while she played Scrabble and checkers and chess with the children—getting to know them even better, falling completely in love with them—Francine's mother plunged into Christmas like a child into a favorite swimming hole, and by December 20, the house smelled like a cookie factory and was alight with color. On the kitchen snack bar she'd stood a three-foot white pine and decked it out in spatulas and spoons trimmed with red gingham ribbons and bows. She'd done up the big Douglas fir in the corner of the living room in a regal angel theme of golds and whites. In the family room, the pointed tip of a fifteen-foot blue spruce scraped the vaulted ceiling. She'd garnished that one with teddy bears and tiny wooden wagons and candy canes; she called it the "children's tree," though Dara failed to understand why, since the kids hadn't been allowed to hang so much as a strand of tinsel and weren't permitted to get within five feet of it now that it was trimmed.

Christmas Eve, as it turned out, was the one-week anniversary of the wedding. Dara thought it would be nice if, after a hearty meal, the family would attend the evening service. Afterward, she'd brew up a kettle of warm and spicy apple cider and serve it with cheese and crackers. She'd packed up her old music books; if she could find them amid the boxes piled in the rented storage cube down on Route 40, maybe they'd gather around the spinet in Noah's living room, sing hymns and carols, the way her parents and grandparents had when she'd been a girl.

The day after the Brewsters arrived, Dara had managed to slip away for an all-in-one shopping trip. It hadn't been necessary to buck Beltway traffic or the crowds in the malls, because everything she needed could be found at the fabric store.

Her first stop had been the design aisle, where she

carefully picked through patterns, searching for just the right things: one little girl's dress, a little boy's blazer, a man's sport coat, five bathrobes in varying styles and sizes, an assortment of vests. Next, she browsed through the colorful bolts of velvet, fleece, flannel and chenille. Then zippers and buttons, thread and lace, topped off the mountain of materials in her shopping cart.

And every night, as the rest of the family snoozed contentedly, Dara tiptoed downstairs to the laundry room, where she'd created an L-shaped sewing center by balancing two unhung doors on sawhorses. The portable machine she'd bought years ago hadn't come equipped with bells and whistles, but it would get the job done.

It had taken all week—two hours here, four hours there—to complete the outfits, and she'd finished every gift with two days to spare! She felt cross-eyed from the eyestrain of burning the midnight oil, working in poor lighting. But she now had the satisfaction of knowing the only thing left to do was wrap the things she'd stitched up, label the packages and arrange them under the family room tree.

After dinner on the twenty-fourth, Dara handed everyone a slice of her deep-dish Dutch apple pie. She didn't wait for compliments...or complaints; instead, she sat on the edge of her chair and made a quiet announcement.

"It was a tradition in my family to make something special for the people you loved." She caught Noah smiling at her, and blushed. "I, ah, I thought it might be nice to blend traditions this year, since I'm so new to the family."

"Sounds like a great idea," Noah said softly. "What do you have in mind?"

"Well, I know this is a little out of the ordinary," she said, choosing her words carefully, "but you're all going to have to open one gift tonight."

"Co-o-o-ol," Bobby said, grinning.

"Neat!" his sister agreed.

"Open gifts before Christmas morning?" Emmaline clucked. "Out of the question!"

"But—"

Bobby's interruption was silenced by his grandmother's raised finger and haughty stare.

Dara had been afraid this might happen, so she'd prepared a speech just in case. "Not everything, Emmaline. Just one of the gifts I've made for each of you."

"*Made* us?" Emmaline put down her dessert fork and sat ramrod straight in her chair. "One of your gifts to us is…is a *handicraft?*"

From the look on her face, Dara thought grimly, you'd think I was wrapping yesterday's potato peels as gifts. "Actually," she began, her smile firmly in place, "everything I'm giving was handmade."

"By you?"

Dara nodded.

Francine's mother rolled her eyes. "Regardless," she huffed, "we *never* open our gifts before Christmas morning." She looked to Noah for support. "Do we, darling?"

He tucked in one corner of his mouth and regarded her for a moment before saying, "Ordinarily, that's true." He met Dara's eyes then and, smiling warmly, added, "You say your family opened one gift apiece on Christmas Eve?"

Another nod...a hopeful one that was mimicked by Angie and Bobby.

"You *are* a part of this family, after all, and I see no reason your traditions can't become part of our traditions." He winked. "When would you like to get started?"

"Now!" Bobby suggested, leaping up from his chair.

"I'm finished with my pie," Angie volunteered, standing beside him.

Emmaline's lips formed a tight, straight line. "This is highly irregular."

Standing beside her, Noah bent down, slipped an arm around her shoulders. "Ease up, Emmie," he said, grinning as he kissed her cheek. "It's *Christmas*, for goodness' sake."

"Not until tomorrow morning it isn't!" She tossed her napkin on top of her uneaten pie. "I let you get away with that nickname when my daughter was alive because she asked me to overlook it. But she's gone now, and I'll thank you to address me by my given name."

Noah straightened, his smile vanishing. His narrowed eyes glittered like blue diamonds as his brows dipped low in the center of his forehead. From all outward appearances, he seemed to be gearing up to raise the roof, and Dara couldn't help but wonder what was going on in that handsome head of his.

Then he pursed his lips and took a deep breath. "I assure you, Emmaline," he said with deliberate slowness, "I meant no disrespect. I'm genuinely sorry if I offended you." He held out one hand and smiled affectionately. "Now, will you join us in the family room?"

He'd handled the matter with gentle aplomb, yet there was no doubt in anyone's mind who was in charge of the situation. The choice he'd given Emmaline was simple: join the family or sit alone in the dining room.

Emmaline's cheeks flushed as she considered her options, and as she fidgeted with the corner of her napkin, it surprised Dara to feel a twinge of pity for the woman. It must have been hard for Emmaline, Dara thought, to lose her daughter and now to see Noah finally starting over again, with a new wife.

A tense moment passed before Francine's mother put her hand into Noah's. "Oh, very well," she muttered. "I read a report just the other day," she continued, clinging to his arm, "that said change keeps us mentally alert, keeps us young." She gabbed all the way into the family room, kept right on chattering until everyone was gathered around the tree. "Well," she sniffed, "we'd better get on with it if we don't want to be late for the Christmas Eve service."

Dara handed Emmaline an artistically wrapped box of iridescent maroon, tied up with a huge, pink satin bow. "This one is for you," she told Francine's mother.

The woman balanced the pretty package on her knees. "Let the children open theirs first." She lifted her chins. "Christmas *is* for children, after all."

Correction, Dara wanted to say, Christmas is for Christ. But she picked up two more boxes, instead. "Here you go, Bobby, Angie."

Giggling and squealing, the kids ripped into the parcels as if they'd never experienced the holiday before. Angie got into hers first and stood. "Oh, Dara." She sighed. "It's so *pretty!*" She pressed the deep green velvet against her and twirled several times, nearly overturning the arrangement of pine-scented green candles and pomegranates in the center of the coffee table. "Look, Father," she gushed, "it has rows and rows of lace, and pearl buttons and a little lady pin on the collar."

"It's called a cameo," Dara said. "It belonged to my grandmother."

Noah's left brow shot up. "You…you gave her a family heirloom?"

"Why not?" she said matter-of-factly. "She's family now, isn't she?"

His smile warmed her all the way to her toes. He focused on his daughter then. "You'll have to take very good care of the pin, sweetie. It's very valuable, and it meant a great deal to Dara."

Angie threw her arms around Dara's waist, squeezed her tight. "Oh, thank you! It's beautiful!"

"I'm glad you like it, sweetie, and I hope the dress fits. I made myself one exactly like it."

Noah took the dress from Angie, held it at arm's length. "This looks store-bought." Admiration glowed in his eyes when he looked at her. "You're amazing, you know that?"

Angie, jumping up and down, said, "Can I wear it to church tonight?"

"*May* I," Bobby corrected, smirking.

Laughing, Dara ruffled his hair. "Pay this little tease no mind, Angie." She kissed the boy's cheek. "And yes, you may wear the dress to church. That's one of the reasons I wanted you to open the present now."

"Oooh, oooh," she chanted, bouncing in place, "may I put it on now, Father. Pul-eeeeze?"

"Let's see what Dara has for the rest of us, first, okay?" he suggested.

She started to pout, but one look at Dara stopped her. Brown eyes gleaming, she smiled. "You're the best mother in the whole world," Angie said, hugging her again. "I love you!"

Biting her lip, Dara returned the girl's hug. "I love you, too," she said as tears filled her eyes.

Bobby held up a sport jacket whose pocket bore the Baltimore Orioles' bird and insignia. "Co-o-o-ol," he said, awestruck. "I won't mind wearing *this* coat to church!" he shouted as Dara handed Joseph his gift.

"A vest?" Francine's father said.

"I noticed your favorite one was a little frayed around the hem." She shrugged. "I tried to find material to match it, but that was the closest I could come."

She watched as the older man ran his hand along the satiny lining.

"You know, I don't believe anyone has ever given me a more thoughtful gift." He rose, crossed to where Dara stood and kissed her cheek. "Thank you. You're a wonder."

While she blushed, Noah said, "You're next, Emmaline."

Almost reluctantly, the woman pulled the wrapping from the box on her lap. When she peeled back the bright-pink tissue paper inside, she emitted a tiny gasp. "A cashmere sweater?" She met Dara's eyes. "Such a shame they're so itchy."

"But, Grandmother," Angie interrupted. "It's just what you've always wanted. You said so last year, remember?"

She raised one eyebrow. "It's very nice," she said stiffly. "The detail is—"

"The detail is simply exquisite," Angie said for her, doing a perfect imitation of her grandmother.

"The detail is quite nice," Emmaline concluded, primly folding the sweater on her lap.

"Aren't you going to put it on, Grandmother?"

She shot Angie a withering gaze. "On Christmas morning. That's the proper time to try on gifts." She aimed a hot stare in Dara's direction. "You say you made this? When did you find the time?"

Dara shrugged. "They sell bolts of knitted fabric these days, it was no big deal, really."

"Your turn, Father," Angie said. "*Please* open your present so I can go upstairs and put on my beautiful new dress."

Chuckling, he did as his daughter asked. "What have we here?" he asked, digging through the tissue paper.

"It's a sport coat just like mine!" Bobby hollered. "We'll be twins, Dad! Isn't that the coolest?"

"You bet," he said as the grandfather clock in the foyer began to chime.

"Six o'clock," Angie announced, grabbing her dress, and dashed toward the stairs. "We'd better hurry up if we don't want to be late!"

"Right," her brother agreed, running after her. "Remember how crowded it was last year?"

Dara met Noah's eyes. "I didn't see you in church last Christmas."

"Well, I saw you."

The heat issuing from his eyes could have ignited a fire, and sent a thrill pulsing through Dara that refused to be doused by the chattering children, the curious stares of Emmaline and Joseph, the gonging clock.

"Last one ready is a rotten egg!" Bobby hollered from the top of the steps.

"Robert, really," Emmaline scolded as she headed upstairs, "must you be so vulgar? What's gotten into you lately, with all this uncouth talk?"

"Uncouth?" Dara repeated lightly. "What on earth do you mean? He's the most polite little boy I've ever met!"

The woman rolled her dark eyes. "'Cool' and 'neat' and now 'rotten egg.'" She aimed a stern stare at her grandson. "You'd better watch your language, young man, or I might just have to wash your mouth out with soap!"

Bobby's blue eyes widened, then filled with tears.

"Grandmother," Angie said, slipping an arm around him, "he's very sensitive. I think you've hurt his feelings."

"Sometimes a little pain is necessary," she said, head high and shoulders back, "to ensure that children will grow up right."

"Say, Emmaline," Dara whispered conspiratorially, winking and smiling, "in honor of the holiday, what do you say we lighten up on the little guys?"

She aimed her steely-eyed gaze at Dara. "I have two things to say to *you*. First of all, I don't recall giving you permission to address me by my first name. And second, I'll thank you not to question my authority in front of the children. They're not blood kin to you, after all." That said, she marched up the stairs, nose in the air, and slammed the guest room door.

Stunned into silence by the stinging tirade, Dara stood, blinking and biting her lips to keep the tears at bay. The woman seems determined to embarrass and humiliate you, she thought, and Noah seems intent to let her. More proof, in her mind, that his strongest loyalties were with Francine and her family.

Joseph, red faced and stuttering, stared after his wife. "They say those midlife mood swings are supposed to diminish once a gal turns sixty or so." He shrugged. "Guess there's an exception to every rule," he said, forcing a grin, "'cause it seems my Emmaline has been goin' through the change for just about as long as I've known her!"

He started for the stairs but laid a hand upon Dara's forearm, instead. "Don't let her get to you," he whispered. "Her bark is worse than her bite." Punctuating his comment with a merry wink, he left her alone with Noah in the foyer.

"We'd better get ready, too," he said, extending his hand. And when Dara put hers into it, he led her up the steps. "When did you have time to make all these outfits?" he asked as they walked.

"I've been getting up...after you fall asleep."

"You *what?* How long have you been doing *that?*"

"Oh, about a week."

He opened their bedroom door. "Seven days, give or take, working in the middle of the night," he said as she entered the room. "Joseph was right," he added, shaking his head. "You're a wonder."

The wonder, she thought as he closed the door, is why I talked you out of sending them packing!

Well, you've made it this far. One more week, and you'll be out of the woods.

Grinning, she thought of all the Christmas trees Emmaline had decorated in the various rooms of the house, because for the first time in her life, she empathized with Little Red Riding Hood....

He'd been thinking about it for nearly two weeks now—how to call Emmaline on the carpet without hurting her too badly, though he didn't for the life of him know why sparing her feelings was so important to him; she hadn't given a thought to what her prickly comments were doing to Dara.

Because, he thought, you may have been brought up in an orphanage, but you were raised better than that.

He recalled the numerous "treat your elders with respect" lectures he'd received from Brother Constantine, one for every time he'd stepped out of line as a boy. "'Rebuke not an elder, but treat him as a father,'" the Brother would recite from First Timothy, "'and the younger men as brethren....'"

The good Brother thought the words had fallen on deaf ears back then, and Noah was inclined to agree. But now the words echoed with the full meaning of the man's intent.

As the kids of the parish filed onstage and took their places in the stereotypical Nativity scene, the idea began to formulate in Noah's brain. While Pete Lang's black lab—outfitted to look like a donkey—was tugging on one of the wise men's robes, Noah knew what to do.

The moment the family returned home from the service, Dara followed the kids upstairs. "I'll just tuck them in," she said, "before I take my bath."

"Sounds good," he told her. To Angie and Bobby, he said, "I'll be up in a bit to hear your prayers."

He waited until Dara was out of earshot to ask Emmaline, "Will you take a walk with me?"

Laughing, Francine's mother waved a hand at Noah. "Don't be ridiculous, darling. It's barely thirty degrees outside!"

"So we'll bundle up good and warm." He held out the full-length mink coat she'd worn to the Christmas Eve service and, like a bullfighter, shook it at the stubborn woman. "Just a short walk," he said, smiling. "It's been a long time since we've had a chance to talk...alone."

"Well, all right," she agreed reluctantly, shrugged into the fur. She wrapped a knitted silk scarf around her neck, pulled fur-lined leather gloves over her hands. "You're just lucky I haven't taken off my boots yet—that's all I can say!"

He pulled open the door, held it as she stepped onto the front porch. It dawned on him as she crossed the doorsill that he hadn't done any of the customary bridegroom things for Dara, like getting down on one knee to ask her to marry him and slipping an engagement ring onto her finger, or carrying her over the threshold. You're going to have to remedy that, soon as possible, he told himself, shutting the door behind them. But first things first.

"Angela and Robert were so excited. Do you think they'll get any sleep tonight at all?" she asked softly, linking her arm with his.

"Eventually. I tell them the same thing every Christmas Eve—the sooner you fall asleep, the sooner it'll be Christmas morning."

Emmaline's laugh vaporized, floated from them on a cloud of cold air. Then, in a more serious tone, she said, "You're a good father, Noah. I know I don't tell you that nearly often enough. Joseph and I think you've been doing a splendid job, raising those youngsters all by yourself."

"I'm not all by myself anymore."

She sighed. "Please. Don't remind me."

Noah stopped walking, put himself directly in his former mother-in-law's path. "Emmaline, that's precisely what I wanted to talk to you about."

"I'm afraid I don't understand."

"Dara is my wife." He cocked his head, gave her an affectionate yet scolding stare. "I don't like the way you've been treating her."

She exhaled a sigh of vexation. "It's just… We were doing fine without that…that…"

"That wonderful woman who's my wife?" he finished for her.

But she seemed not to have heard him. "Why didn't you call me before you let her steamroller you into a wedding you weren't ready for, Noah. I mean, really…a six-week courtship? Honestly, what *were* you thinking!"

"Steamroller me?" He had to laugh. "Emmaline, if only you knew."

"Why do I get the feeling," she said starchily, "that you're about to tell me."

He smiled. "I never gave it a thought to call you, to tell the truth. I met her and I fell for her like a load of bricks. Besides," he added for good measure, "I figured it was high time I did what Francine told me to do on the night she died."

"Surely you don't expect me to believe she *asked* you to replace her!"

"That's exactly what she did. And frankly," he said, smile still in place, "I don't give a hoot what you believe."

He ignored her light gasp. "Your daughter realized the importance of a mother's love in her children's lives, and she made me swear to see that they got it."

"There's no need to take that tone with me, Noah," she huffed. "I was only—"

There's *every* reason to take this tone, he told her mentally.

"I know you were only trying to help," he said, finishing her sentence. And nodding, he added, "And I appreciate your concern—really I do."

"Then I don't understand." She thrust out her lower lip, tucked her chins into her coat collar. "Why are you scolding me?"

There were tears in her eyes, but Noah refused to react to them. He'd seen her pull this stunt many times, mostly with her husband and daughter; somewhere along the line, she'd figured out that if her temper didn't get the result she wanted, a crying jag just might do the trick.

Unfortunately, it was a lesson Francine had learned at Emmaline's knee. Well, Noah thought, it was dishonest and mean the way some women used their feminine wiles to get their way. If they wanted something, why not ask for it straight out?

"I'm not being *half* as hard on you as you've been on Dara since you got to town."

She stopped blotting her eyes long enough to say, "Hard on her? Why, I've been nothing but pleasant and kind to that young woman. Which, if you ask me, is quite a feat, considering—"

"Considering *what*? Francine has been gone almost four years now. The kids need a mother. I need a wife. And Dara, believe it or not, needs *us*."

She gave a disapproving snort. "She's getting quite

a deal if you ask me…a highly respected husband with a successful business, a lovely home filled with beautiful furniture, two wonderful children.…''

"*We're* the ones getting the 'deal.'''

A moment of tense silence ticked by. "I think it's important that the kids have as much contact with you and Joseph as possible. You're the only grandparents they'll ever have, after all, but we have to figure out how we're going to get along around here. Otherwise, everyone is going to be miserable, and after a while, nobody is going to want to see anybody. And you know who's gonna pay if that happens?''

She looked at the toes of her boots. "I don't see what any of this has to do with anything.''

"The children will pay,'' he finished.

"Did I hear you correctly? Dara's mother and father are dead?''

"Yes. And if you ask me, I think she was hoping the two of you would hit it off so she could look to you and Joseph as substitute parents.''

Emmaline pursed her lips and gave that some serious consideration. "Well,'' she began, "of course Dara could never replace Francine in my heart.''

"She isn't trying to replace her, not in *your* heart, not in mine, not in Angie's or Bobby's.'' He gave Emmaline an affectionate hug. "Won't you at least try to see it from her point of view? She was a bride barely more than a day when you arrived. I mean, think about it—the parents of her new husband's deceased wife? How would you feel in her place?''

"Scared out of my socks,'' she admitted.

"And it only makes matters worse when you constantly hold Francine up as an example of the 'Perfect Wife.'''

"I suppose you have a point. The poor girl can't hold a candle to my daughter, but that isn't her fault, now is it? She *is* trying." She shook her head. "Can you believe those gifts!"

"She's a treasure, all right."

Emmaline said nothing.

"So you'll help me?"

"Help you what?"

"Help me make Dara feel welcome. There won't be any more complaining. No more snide remarks about her cooking and housekeeping. No more interfering with her disciplining of—"

"Discipline! You call what she's doing *disciplining?* Noah, she'll mollycoddle those youngsters if you don't make her take a stronger stand. 'Spare the rod, spoil the child,' the Good Book says. You mark my words," she said, shaking a finger at him, "Angela and Robert need a firm hand and guidance. And who does she think she is, anyway, marching in here like Queen of the May!"

"She's my wife," he began. Noah ran a hand through his hair and prayed for strength, for guidance of his own. "The kids need a mother's love," he said at last. "They need *Dara.*"

She stared stubbornly straight ahead.

"You know how much I love you, Emmaline, but—"

"And I couldn't love you more if you were my own son."

"But Dara is my *wife.*" He gave her hands another squeeze. "All I ask is that you treat her with respect." He paused and, grinning, said, "She could learn a lot from you, if only you'd teach the lessons with a little tact."

She looked up at him, blinking in honest surprise. "All right, darling. I'll be nice to your little wife if it'll make you happy."

Noah hugged her. "It'll make me happy. Very happy."

"Now, let's go inside," she said, patting his cheek affectionately, "I'm freezing!"

Her condo had been on the market only one day when the first couple to do a walk-through bought it. Her parents' house had been in the multiple list computer only eight days when it sold. Dara had never seen more money in one place at one time. Shaking her head, she stared at her bank statement. Between her savings and the proceeds from the houses, the total beside the colon on the "this is your balance" line read $315,655.72.

More than enough to pay back the money Dad took from the Pinnacle account...and the capital gains taxes to boot, she thought, smiling with relief. Grabbing her coat and car keys, she dashed into the kitchen, where Noah and his former in-laws and the children were having a midmorning Saturday snack. "Will you be around for a while?"

"Sure." Noah gave her a puzzled look. "Why? Where are you off to in such a hurry?"

"I, ah, I have a few errands to run." She smiled at the kids. "How about if I pick up a pizza on my way home?"

"Pepperoni and mushroom?" Angie asked.

"Tell 'em extra sauce!" Bobby put in.

She pressed a kiss to each of their foreheads, then ran out the door, breathless and anxious and feeling better about what her father had done than she had since Noah had dropped the bombshell on her all those weeks ago.

Halfway to the bank, as she sat at the red light at Route 40 and Centennial Lane, her spirited mood died a quick death. How are you going to put the money into the Pinnacle account, she asked herself, when you don't even have a deposit slip?

When the light turned green, she eased away from the intersection, brow furrowed in thought. Maybe there's something in Dad's office…an old checkbook or a statement with the account number on it.

She nosed the car into a space in the Pinnacle lot and fished her key ring from her purse. Her father had given her the keys to the company years ago, when he'd been laid up with a broken leg and couldn't get into the office. Pinnacle's building was right on her way home from work and halfway between the school and her parents' house. So she'd stopped in, going and coming, to deliver messages to and from her dad.

He had been a man who hated change, so she'd fully expected to find the checkbook still in the narrow center drawer of his desk. What she found, instead, staggered her.

The name engraved on the brass plate tacked to the door said William Prentice, CFO. Dara had never even *heard* of a William Prentice, so how could he have replaced her father?

She knocked on the door, shoved it open a crack when no one answered. Stepping inside, she tiptoed closer to the desk—her *father's* desk—and breathed a sigh of relief. Everything looks just as it did the last time I was here, she thought, right down to the plaque on the wall.

So this William Prentice person must not have

moved in yet. She couldn't believe her good fortune! Dara walked around behind the desk, slid open the center drawer.

Empty.

She opened the deeper file drawer to its right.

Empty.

And so were the filing cabinets and the credenza.

"May I help you?"

Dara spun around so quickly she nearly toppled over. "Mr. Turner!" she heaved. "You scared me half to death!"

"Good to see you, Dara. It's been quite a while."

Since Dad's funeral, to be exact.

"I suppose you're here to pack up your father's things."

It was as good an excuse as any to be on Pinnacle property on a Saturday morning, so Dara nodded.

He frowned slightly. "Wait a minute. Didn't you…" Tucking in one corner of his gray-bearded mouth, he said, "Didn't you gather up his things months ago?"

"I—I packed a few things, yes, yes," she stammered. "But I—I didn't get everything." She grabbed the plaque from the wall. "This, for example."

Turner's green gaze scanned the tweedy carpet. "I don't see any packing boxes."

"I, ah, this was all I really wanted," she said, hugging it to her. "It's all right if I take it, isn't it?"

He smiled suspiciously. "Of course it's all right."

"Well, then," she said, sidestepping toward the door, "I guess I'll be on my way. It was good seeing you again, Mr.—"

"I hear you married the head of our accounting firm."

He wasn't smiling when he said it, and Dara didn't

understand the angry gleam burning in his green eyes. "That's right," she said lightly. "December 18."

"Congratulations. I hope you'll be very happy."

"I'm sure we will," she said, turning to go. "Well, as I said, I have a lot to do."

"Did you make yourself a list?"

She stopped in the doorway. "Excuse me?"

"Your father used to talk about you all the time— about how you never went anywhere without a list of 'things to do.'" He drew quotation marks in the air.

It was true. She *did* make lists, for practically everything. But she hadn't made one this morning.

"I guess your lists are longer than ever these days, eh, what with Noah and his kids to take care of. You probably have *thousands* of things written down."

Why had he accented the number so harshly? she wondered.

"I imagine Noah helps you itemize things, so that not even one of those thousands of things will slip through the cracks."

Dara believed she knew why Turner had put special emphasis on the word: her father's ex-partner suspected *her* of having had something to do with the missing money, and because she'd married Noah, *he* was a suspect, too. Dara's heart thundered. It was bad enough that the theft had tarnished Jake's once-good name, but for his actions to have an effect on Noah's stellar reputation...

Oh, Daddy, she thought dismally, what have you done!

"I hate to spring this on you now," Dara said. She sat at her dressing table, brushing her hair. Noah was laying on the bed, still in his clothes, reading a book.

"Uh-oh, sounds like bad news." He looked up from his book.

"I'm afraid it is." She took a deep breath and turned to look at him. "I went to Pinnacle Construction today."

He walked over to her and slipped his arm around her shoulders. "Aw, sweetie. Why didn't you tell me? I'd have gone with you." He kissed her forehead. "Couldn't have been easy. Today was the eight-month anniversary of your father's death, wasn't it?"

It surprised her more than a little to discover he'd kept track of something so important to her.

"So what did you do—pack up the last of his personal stuff?"

"No. I wanted to get a deposit slip."

Noah pulled back slightly, brow crinkled in confusion. "A deposit slip?"

She exhaled. "Well, you know that the real-estate checks came in for the sale of my condo and Mom and Dad's house."

One blond brow rose on his forehead. "Uh-huh."

"When I left here this morning, it was my intention to put that two hundred thousand back."

"But…but I thought you were going to let *me* do that."

He was *really* puzzled now. She could see it in the furrow of his brow, the tautness of his lips, could hear it in his usually resonant voice. She rose to face him and gently brushed a strand of hair from his eyes. "That was the plan, but I changed my mind."

He tucked a curl behind her ear. "Why?"

"Because," she admitted, "I don't want that money hanging over our heads for the rest of our lives."

"Hanging over…" Noah placed his hands on her

shoulders. "Wait just a minute here. You don't really believe I'd use the money as a weapon...do you?"

"Of course not."

"I was only waiting till after the first of the year to return the money, so I could say I'd found it while filling out the company's quarterly tax report. I hope you didn't think I was procrastinating because I'd changed my mind."

"No." She smiled softly. "No, I've always known you'd keep your end of the bargain. I just don't think it's fair for you to have to right my father's wrongs."

"Bargain?" Noah clapped a hand over his eyes. "Dara, sweetie, you talk as if I think of our marriage as nothing more than a business deal." He shook his head. "That isn't what you think." He winced. "Is it?"

"Not exactly. I—"

He gazed down at her with a solemn expression. His deep voice trembled. "I've made a lot of mistakes in my life. I don't want to make *any* where you're concerned. You have to believe me when I say this marriage means more to me than that." He paused, his gaze darkened. "A lot more."

But you can't make yourself say you love me, can you? "I need your help, Noah."

"What kind of help?"

"I don't have access to the company checkbook, but you do. And the more I think about it, the more confused I get. I mean, the real-estate money is in my savings account. If I write a personal check and deposit it in the Pinnacle account..." Exasperated, she took a deep breath. "And if I go to my bank, ask them to print out a cashier's check for two hundred thousand dollars, payable to Pinnacle, won't someone eventually be able to trace it back to my account? How do I put the money back without drawing attention to us?''

''Us?''

She nodded again. ''Kurt Turner caught me in Dad's office. It was pretty clear that he thought I had something to do with those missing funds. And,'' she added, sighing, ''now that we're married, he's suspicious of you, too.''

''He said that?''

''Not in so many words.''

''I see.''

''I *have* to put that money back, as quickly as possible.'' She grasped his hand, gave it a squeeze. ''You've just *got* to help me to figure out a way it can be done without putting you at risk.''

''Tell you what,'' he said, drawing her close, ''why don't you just let me handle this alone?''

She snuggled against his chest, shaking her head. ''No. Absolutely not. That's out of the question. This is my responsibility, not yours.'' She shrugged. ''It's my fault you're involved in this mess in the first place. I wouldn't have bothered you with it at all if I knew more about banking and…and whatnot.''

He kissed her forehead. ''Okay. I'll fill you in on the 'whatnots,' if it'll make you feel better, but—''

She threw her arms around him, kissed him soundly. ''Oh, Noah,'' she gushed, ''thank you. Thank you so much!''

Chuckling, he said, ''If *this* is what I'll get for digging you out of jams, I hope you'll be in trouble a lot!'' Then, on a more serious note, he added, ''I'll help you on one condition.''

Dara looked into his eyes, heart pounding with love for this kindhearted, beautiful man. ''What condition?''

"That you'll never shut me out again. Not for any reason. Promise?"

"I promise."

"Okay. First thing Monday morning, I'll get to work. By start of business Tuesday, the case of the missing money will be solved."

He wrapped her in his arms and rested his chin atop her head. "How does that sound?" he asked.

She felt safe in his embrace, so protected and secure. "It sounds perfect," she replied.

And you're a perfect husband, she reflected. No wonder I love you.

Chapter Twelve

Frank Howard shook Noah's hand, invited him to have a seat on one of the bloodred leather wingbacks across from his burled mahogany desk. "Good thing for Pinnacle," he drawled, sitting in his many-tufted black chair, "that they found a way to pay off that debt at the eleventh hour."

Noah slid the envelope bearing the check from his briefcase and faced the big Texan. "What do you mean?"

"Well, it's suspicious, don't you think, that the whole time we've been talkin' lawsuits, they've been cryin' bankruptcy. Then the day before the fifty-thousand-dollar late fee kicks in, they cough up the whole kit an' kaboodle. Tells me they had the resources to pay up the whole time...and they were stringin' us along!"

"Well, no harm no foul," Noah stated. "Besides, it's not so strange, really," he went on. "Companies do it all the time. You probably do it yourself, to keep that interest money rolling in till the last possible minute.''

"No, I don't, either!'' His fist thumped the desktop. "My daddy raised me to pay my debts in full and on time. It's one of the principles this country was founded on, one of the reasons Howard Equipment is the biggest company of its kind.''

Noah nodded politely as the older gent retold the story he'd told a hundred times before, about how his great-great-grandfather, a blacksmith, settled in Texas territory and built a burgeoning business from nothing but hard work and good intentions.

"I don't cotton to folks makin' a profit off of unethical business practices. The money they make comes outta *my* pocket, confound 'em!''

"I agree,'' Noah said, meaning it, "but I'm Pinnacle's accountant, not their collective conscience.'' He handed Howard the check and, standing, said, "I have a favor to ask you, Frank.''

He tore open the envelope, peered inside at the check. "This thing won't bounce, will it?''

Chuckling, Noah shook his head. "Not a chance. That money has been sitting in a special account, earmarked for this payment.''

Scowling, he slapped the envelope onto his desktop. "So what's this favor you want, Lucas?''

"Can you nudge your accounts receivable department a little? Get them to send off a 'paid in full' statement ahead of schedule?''

He stood behind the desk, leaned his knuckles on the blotter. "Why in tarnation should I do that?'' he thundered.

Noah took a deep breath. "Well, I don't suppose you heard, but I just got married, and—''

"Is that right?" The big Texan strode around to the front of his desk, pumped Noah's arm up and down like a pump handle. "Well, congratulations, boy! You have young'uns to raise, ain't that right?"

He nodded. "Two of them, a girl and a boy."

"How old are they?" Howard asked, perching on the corner of his desk.

"Angie is seven, and Bobby is six."

Crossing both arms over his chest, Howard chuckled and shook his head. "Got me grandkids older than that!"

"So as I was saying," Noah continued, "I've been a little distracted these past few weeks, what with the wedding and—"

"Say no more," Howard bellowed, laughing. "I'll head on downstairs and have Mable type one up soon as we're through here, get 'em to mail that statement right off to the folks at Pinnacle. We'll protect your purty li'l self, all right...."

Noah extended his hand. "Thanks, Frank. I don't usually let things like this fall through the cracks."

"Boy," the Texan said, "if you *weren't* distracted by a new bride, I'd say there was somethin' wrong with you!"

"You're a lifesaver. I mean that."

Howard's ruddy cheeks reddened even more in response. He clapped a fatherly hand on Noah's shoulder. "Now, git on outta here, boy, so you can clock out on time, have a cozy l'il dinner with that new wife of yours."

Noah felt a little guilty, having misled Frank that way. But he took comfort in the fact that he'd done nothing unethical or dishonest. Rather, everything had been completely aboveboard, from the cash deposit he'd made with Dara's money into Pinnacle's account, to the bank check he'd had drafted in the amount of two hundred thousand, made payable to Howard Equipment.

When Frank's accounting department forwarded the statement to Pinnacle, all parties concerned would believe Jake Mackenzie had had the foresight—before his trip to England—to earmark funds that would honor the company's debt…just in time to save *another* fifty grand in penalties. Not only would he be cleared of any suspicion of embezzlement, he'd go down in company history as the man who'd given his life to save Pinnacle Construction.

Buoyed by the knowledge that her father's good name had been preserved, Noah gunned the motor of his car and steered into traffic. He couldn't wait to get home and tell his wife the good news.

Dara couldn't explain Emmaline's behavior. Ever since Christmas Eve, she'd been strangely quiet, and it seemed the woman had been deliberately avoiding her.

They were in the kitchen together—Dara standing at the sink, washing dishes; Emmaline perched on a stool at the snack bar, peeling potatoes—when Angie and Bobby skipped into the room.

"Can I have a sugar cookie?" the boy wanted to know.

She gave him a crooked smile. "Well, I suppose it won't hurt to have just one."

"Me, too?" Angie asked.

Dara winked. "Why not."

Emmaline sighed heavily—a sure sign she didn't approve of Dara's permissiveness. But she wasn't about to ask the woman to state her opinions on the subject. Life is too short! she thought, grinning to herself.

The children helped themselves to one cookie apiece and slid onto stools to eat them. Bobby pressed his palm to the snack bar, rested his chin on the back of his hand. "This sure would taste good with a big ole glass of milk," he teased, mischievously wiggling his eyebrows when Dara looked his way.

"Goodness, Bobby," she said, grabbing a glass from the cupboard. "You're so subtle that—"

"Subtle indeed," Emmaline complained. "All this indulgence around here is turning him into a rude little rascal."

"What's a rascal?" Bobby whispered to Angie.

"A brat," she whispered back.

"I'm not a brat, Grandmother."

"That's a matter of opinion."

"But I'm a good kid." He looked at Dara. "Right?"

She opened her mouth to agree, but Emmaline beat her to the punch.

"If you were as good as you think," his grandmother said, "maybe God wouldn't have sent you to the hospital."

He looked into his grandmother's eyes, tears filling his own. And without a word, he slid from his stool and ran from the room.

Angie shot Emmaline an angry look, then ran after her brother. "Bobby," she called, "wait up."

Dara calmly dried her hands on a dish towel and walked purposefully toward the snack bar. "Mrs. Brewster," she said, sitting on the stood beside Francine's mother, "we have to talk."

Emmaline put down her paring knife, wiped her hands on her apron. "About what?"

"About what just went on in here." Dara hung her heels on the stool's bottom rung, rested her hands on jeans-clad knees. "I've been quiet when you chewed me up one side and down the other, but I can't sit idly by while you belittle the children. Especially when they've done nothing wrong."

"Nothing wrong!" Emmaline protested. "Why, they're becoming little barbarians!"

Noah had decided to stop off at home on his way back to the office, rather than phone Dara with the news about the payment. He'd let himself in through the front door and headed toward the sound of voices in the kitchen. He'd stopped short of the doorway, though, when Emmaline's scolding drove his children from the room.

"They're not barbarians," he heard Dara say. "They're terrific kids. And you have to stop ridiculing them." She paused. "They were so excited—no, make that *thrilled*—when they heard you were coming for Christmas. Don't you know how much they love you?"

"Of course they love me," she scoffed. "I'm their grandmother."

"Then may I suggest you act like one and warm up a little. Spend some time with Angie and Bobby—not teaching them how to bow and curtsy, but getting to *know* them."

"What kind of nonsense is this? I've known them all their lives!"

"If you knew them, *really* knew them, Mrs. Brewster, you'd realize what remarkable children they are."

"I don't have to sit here and listen to this," she said, starting to get off the stool.

"You're absolutely right. But you *do* have to stop being so mean to the kids." She held a hand in the air to forestall Emmaline's retort. "I realize I'm not their natural-born mother, but I love them as much as if they were mine. It hurts them when you call them names, and I'll do whatever I must to keep them from being hurt."

Emmaline gasped. "Why, of all the… I'd never hurt them. How dare you insinuate such a thing!"

"Mrs. Brewster, I'm not *insinuating* anything." Frustrated, she sighed. "I know you don't like me, but that's a problem only if we can't learn to work around it…for the kids' sake."

"I never said I didn't like you."

Dara snickered quietly. "Well, you sure could have fooled me!"

Noah leaned back so that he could see them but they couldn't see him.

He watched Emmaline begin to pace, from the sink to the stove to the snack bar and back again.

"It isn't you, don't you see? It's me!"

"What do you mean?"

Emmaline stopped, faced Dara and said, "Everyone loves you. Noah, the children—even Joseph thinks the world of you. It's Dara this and Dara that. You'd think you hung the moon!"

In all the years he'd known her, Noah had never seen the woman cry for real, but her tears were genuine now.

"You're not the perfect housekeeper or a prizewinning cook," she blubbered, "but you don't *need* to be perfect." She threw her hands into the air. "Don't you see, they love you just for yourself!"

Dara nodded slowly, telling Noah that she was getting the same picture he had gotten: Emmaline was *jealous* of Dara!

She slid off her stool and drew Emmaline into a

warm hug. "You're sadly mistaken if you think they don't love you, Mrs. Brewster. They're crazy about you—Noah, the kids—and Mr. Brewster adores you. Anyone with eyes and ears knows it!" Patting the older woman's back, she added, "No one expects you to be perfect, least of all the bunch of us. We're family, for goodness' sake! If you can't relax with us, who *can* you be yourself with?"

Emmaline stepped out of Dara's embrace, blotted her eyes on a corner of her apron. "Joseph was right," she said, sniffing.

"About what?"

Impulsively, she grabbed Dara's hand. "You're a wonder."

And Noah, from his vantage point, nodded in agreement. He'd loved her from first sight, but never more than right now.

The next weeks flew by in a flurry of activity, with Dara volunteering at the elementary school and putting the finishing touches on the house.

She'd always been a bundle of energy, so the fact that she'd been tiring by suppertime worried her more than a little. Perhaps caring for Noah and the children, as well as all the holiday preparations and entertaining Joseph and Emmaline, had worn down her usual energy reserves. She'd scheduled a physical, to make sure everything was A-OK.

As it turned out, her appointment was at ten o'clock on Valentine's Day. She'd waited the customary thirty minutes beyond the set time, then sat another ten minutes in the examining room, waiting for Dr. Peterson.

"Sorry I'm late," he said when he breezed into the

room. "I had to break some bad news to my last patient. Took a little longer than I expected."

"Don't worry about it," she said, putting aside the magazine she'd been reading. "Sitting around in here has been the most leisure time I've had in weeks."

He peered at her over the rims of his half glasses, then patted her hand. "I can always count on you to brighten my day, can't I?" He scribbled something in her file, then motioned for her to sit on the edge of the table. "So what's this I hear about you getting married?"

Nodding happily, Dara smiled. "December 18."

"Do I know the lucky fella?"

"I doubt it. His name is Noah Lucas."

Peterson squinted one eye as he palpated Dara's throat. "Can't say as the name is familiar." He plugged the stethoscope into his ears and listened to her chest. "Deep breath now," he instructed. "Now, then," he continued, listening to her back, "what seems to be the trouble?"

"Well, I'm just so *tired* all the time."

He unplugged the stethoscope and grabbed his flashlight. Brow furrowed, he stared into Dara's right eye, then her left. "Are you getting enough rest?"

"I should say so! I'm asleep by eleven and don't get up till six."

"Overdoing it around the house, then?" he asked, strapping the blood pressure cuff into place.

"No, just the usual chores, but Noah's kids are a big help in that department."

He made another note in her file. "Flat on your back, young lady."

Once she was settled, he poked and prodded at her

abdomen. "Hmm," he said, frowning. "Excuse me for a minute, will you?"

Peterson hurried out the door, white coat flapping, and returned with the results of her blood and urine tests. "How long did you say you've been married?"

"Almost two months to the day."

Nodding, he said, "That's right. December 18." He wrote something else in her file. "Go ahead and get dressed," he said. "You know where to find me." With a grin and a wink, he was gone.

Dara hurried into her clothes and rushed right into Peterson's office. He'd been her doctor ever since she was a child. He'd removed her tonsils when she was six. Set her broken arm that time she'd fallen off the monkey bars in the fifth grade. Prescribed antibiotics to get her ear infection under control when she was on the high-school swim team. And performed every other examination—healthy and sick—in between. Settling into the low-backed chair across from his desk, she waited for him to complete his additions to her file.

Peterson removed his half glasses. "How long have we known each other?" he asked, lying them atop the file.

"Well, I'll be thirty in May. Mom brought me to see you for the first time when I was in kindergarten."

"Ah, yes," he said, nodding and smiling, "when you nearly lopped off your big toe in the frog pond at Centennial Park."

Dara laughed at the memory. "I'd almost forgotten about that!"

"You make me feel old, I don't mind telling you."

"Why?"

"Because I doctored you when you were barely

more than a baby, and there you sit, having a baby of your own.''

It took a moment or two for the news to sink in. Dara repeated his words in her head: *a baby of your own. A baby of your own!*

"It's perfectly normal to feel tired, especially during the first trimester. But you're healthy, and you're young. I think you'll be fine, just fine." He grabbed his ballpoint pen and a sheet of prescription paper. "I want you to call this guy," he said, scribbling another doctor's name. "He's one of the best obstetricians in the Baltimore area. He's busy, but he'll make room for you if you tell him I sent you." Peterson tore off the paper, handed it to Dara.

She accepted it with a trembling hand.

"You really had no idea?"

She shook her head. "I thought... There were signs, but I blamed them on nerves. You know, being a new-lywed, adjusting to married life, taking care of two active—"

"Stepchildren?"

"I don't like that term," she said gently. "Active *children.* I like that much better."

"I assume from the way you're glowing, it's good news."

"Very good news," she said, grinning.

Standing, Peterson opened his office door. "Doc Johnston is a great guy. He'll want to see you once a month, every month, until the third trimester. Then he'll play it by ear."

Nodding, Dara walked beside him down the hall.

"He'll bump up the visits at the end, from once a month to every two weeks. And that last month, he'll want to see you every single week." He dropped a fatherly hand on her shoulder. "Gimme a call now and then to let me know how things are going, okay?"

She smiled. "I will."

He stood at the next examining room door. "And drink plenty of milk."

Grinning from ear to ear, Dara pressed a palm to her stomach. A baby, she thought. You're going to have a baby!

She hurried through the waiting room and across the parking lot. *Lord,* she prayed, driving away from the medical building, *help me keep my mind on the road, because I don't think my powers of concentration are going to be too good on the drive home.*

She couldn't wait to get there so she could phone Noah and tell him the news.

It was all she could do to control herself through dinner, through the kids' homework session, through the hour of TV they were allowed to watch before bedtime. They'd worked out a routine in the weeks since Emmaline and Joseph had left—Noah would tuck Bobby in while she listened to Angie's prayers, then they'd trade off.

Dara finished up first and went downstairs to wait for him in the family room. She'd fixed a special dinner in honor of Valentine's Day, complete with fresh flowers on the table, and had made all of Noah's favorites: breaded cubed steaks with roasted potatoes and carrots, spinach salad and a heart-shaped chocolate cake for dessert.

She'd bought him a card, too, and planned to give it to him, along with the tiny box of chocolates she'd bought at the grocery store, when he finished with the children. Her heart hammered when she heard his stocking feet thudding down the stairs. *Please, Lord Jesus,* she prayed, eyes shut tight, hands clenched, *let him be happy about the baby; let him be happy about the baby!*

He didn't come straight into the family room, as she'd expected. She heard the hall closet door open and close. And then, there he was, standing in the doorway, hands clasped behind him, framed by the hallway light.

"Dinner was terrific," he told her.

"So you said...about a hundred and fifty times." She smiled. "So thank you, for the hundred and fiftieth time."

There was a slight crinkling sound as he walked toward her, which intensified when he sat beside her on the sofa. "I wasn't sure what to get you," he began, as one corner of his mouth lifted in a playful grin. "But you don't strike me as the dozen-red-roses type."

"Actually," she said, "I prefer daisies."

His smile doubled in size when he handed her a huge bouquet...of long-petaled white daisies.

"Noah," she gushed, "how did you know?"

He shrugged. "Honest?"

"Honest."

"I have no idea."

They shared a moment of quiet laughter, then she handed him the little box of candy. "I know how much you like chocolate butter creams," she explained, laying the card and candy box between them on the sofa.

"That reminds me," he said, looking at it, sliding a card from his back pocket. He'd folded it in half so it would fit, and he grimaced at it now. "Sorry," he said, holding it out to her. "Guess I'm not much of a romantic."

"Oh, I don't know," she said, accepting it. "Any

guy who buys his girl her favorite posies on Valentine's Day is pretty romantic, in my opinion.''

They read their cards, and hugged and thanked each other, and then Noah popped a chocolate into his mouth. "Mmm," he said around it. "Want one?"

She shook her head. "No, thanks. I'm going to have to start watching what I eat."

His brow crinkled. "Why? You have a terrific figure."

"For now...."

"What?"

She stood, headed for the kitchen. "I'm going to put these in water."

"I'll come with you."

She rooted around in the cabinet under the sink, where she'd stored the vases. After filling one with tap water, she unwrapped the daisies. "I have something to tell you," she said, plucking withered leaves from the stems.

"What a coincidence. I have something to tell you, too."

One by one, she arranged the flowers in the vase. "You go first."

"Okay, if you insist." He led her across the room, where a battered wooden box stood on the table. "I found this while I was searching for a way to clear your father's name," he explained.

"Clear his..." She met his eyes. "Oh, Noah! It's over? You made the payment, and—"

"Yes, sweetie," he said. "It's over. But that isn't the best news." He nodded at the box. "Open it."

She opened it and looked at its contents. Puzzled by the brown leather book on top, she picked it up. "I didn't know Dad kept a journal," she said, frowning.

He took it from her, opened to the page he'd marked with a slip of yellow paper. "You can read the rest later," he said, handing it back to her. "But first, I want you to read this passage."

Dara sat down, laid the book on the table and began to read as Noah stood beside her. She was silent for a long time after closing the book. And then her gaze met Noah's. "He did it for Mom." She sighed. "For *Mom!*"

Not satisfied with the doctors' prognosis, Jake had made it his full-time job to find a way to save his wife. He'd surfed the Net, interviewed cancer specialists all over the world, read every book he could get his hands on, as evidenced by the entries Noah had marked. They had one last chance, as Jake saw it, to save Anne...an experimental treatment being developed in England. But it was costly, and added to all Anne's other medical expenses, Jake didn't have the funds.

And so he'd borrowed the money from the Pinnacle account. Had written an IOU that detailed the amount of the loan, the date the money had been withdrawn and his plans to replace the funds by selling stocks and bonds. Evidently, worry over Anne's quickly failing health distracted him, because the IOU never got delivered; it lay there now, pressed between the pages of his journal, as it had for months.

He'd made the final entry in the diary on the morning he'd left for that last trip to England, to secure Pinnacle that corporate-saving deal with Acmic Chemicals. The experimental treatments had failed to help Anne and had only succeeded in increasing Jake's medical bills. "The minute I get back from London," he'd written, "I'll start selling off stocks and bonds to repay Pinnacle's loan."

He never said why he hadn't asked Kurt Turner straight out to make him the loan. Hadn't said why he'd never mentioned his plans to anyone. Male pride? she wondered. Fear?

But what did it matter now?

Her father *wasn't* a thief! *That* was the only important thing.

He hadn't exactly gone about taking the loan in the most aboveboard way, but she knew him. If he had said he intended to put it back, then he would have put it back. If he had lived. If he was guilty of anything, it was false pride.

The tears that had filled her eyes when she'd started reading the journal abated, and she blew her nose on a paper napkin. "What a relief." She sighed shakily. "What a blessed relief!"

"C'mere," Noah said, taking her hand. She rose and walked into his outstretched arms.

"Thank you, Noah," she whispered, kissing him.

"For what?"

"For…" She looked into his eyes and, smiling, said, "For being you, that's all. Just for being you."

He grinned modestly and shook his head.

"There's something in my shirt pocket for you. But I'm not a romantic, remember, I didn't wrap it."

"Another present?" She giggled. "Noah, you're going to spoil me." She slipped her hand into the pocket, came out with a small, maroon velvet pouch.

"Go on," he coaxed. "Open it."

She tugged at the gold drawstring and peered inside, and when she shook it, a tiny cube of tissue paper landed on her upturned palm. She peeled the paper away…

And exposed a sparkling diamond engagement ring.

"Noah!" she gasped. "What have you done!"

"I've fallen in love with you, that's what." He stood her on her feet, then gently pushed her onto the seat of the chair he'd just vacated. Down on one knee, he took her hand. "Dara Mackenzie," he whispered, boring deep into her eyes, "will you do me the honor of becoming my wife?"

Her eyes filled with tears and, smiling, she nodded.

Noah slipped the ring onto her finger. "Good," he said. "I was worried it wouldn't fit."

She shook her head.

"What?"

"Say it again."

Grinning mischievously, he said, "I was worried it wouldn't fit."

"Not that, silly!"

"Oh. That." He swallowed. "Will you do me the honor of—"

She gave his shoulder a playful shove. "Not that, either!"

He got onto both knees, drew her close. "I love you," he said, lips grazing hers.

Nestled in the crook of his neck, she said, "I love you, too."

"Is that what you wanted to tell me?"

"That was part of it."

"What is the other part?" he said, holding her at arm's length.

"I went to the doctor's today, and—"

Alarm widened his eyes and he gripped her shoulders. "Dara, sweetie. Are you all right? What's wrong?"

"Nothing is wrong, Noah. I went to see Dr. Peterson

to find out why I've been feeling tired lately, that's all.''

"Tired? Does he know why? Did he do tests? What did he say?"

Bracketing his face with both hands, she smiled as tears filled her eyes. "He said I'm going to have a baby."

"A wha— A *baby?*"

She nodded.

"When?"

"September 21, give or take a few days."

There were tears in his eyes, too, when he said, "Aw, sweetie." Noah pressed a palm to her tummy. "A baby? Really?"

"Really."

"If it's a boy," he said, kissing the tip of her nose, "I want to name him Ben."

"Okay. But why?"

"That was Brother Constantine's first name." He kissed her chin.

She nodded. "It's a good, strong name. I like it." Tilting her head, she asked, "But what if it's a girl?"

"I dunno." He kissed her forehead. "Any suggestions?"

"As a matter of fact, I have a few ideas."

He kissed her cheeks. "And they are..."

"Emma, in honor of Emmaline."

"Emma. Nice and old-fashioned and feminine. It's settled, then."

And without warning, he scooped her into his arms and headed for the front door. He flung it open, then deposited her on the porch.

"Noah Lucas," she said, laughing, "what are you doing?"

"I told you once…I've made a lot of mistakes in my past. I don't want to make any where you're concerned." He picked her up again and looked deep into her eyes. "If I wasn't such an insensitive lout, I would have done this on our wedding night."

He stepped over the threshold, then kissed her, full on the lips. "There." He kicked the door shut, then carried her upstairs and laid her on their bed. "Now the only thing left to do is take you on a honeymoon."

"Sweetie, that's very romantic, but I'm afraid that's going to have to wait," she said, patting her stomach.

"Nope. It's all arranged. We leave this weekend."

"What? But what about the kids?"

"Emmaline and Joseph are coming to stay with them for the week." He stretched out beside her, pulled her close.

"Where are we going?"

"It's a surprise."

"But how will I know what to pack?"

"Hmm," he said, scratching his chin. "You've got a point." He nuzzled her throat. "How about that pretty white nightgown you wore on our wedding night?"

"Okay. What else?"

He looked longingly into her eyes. "I can't think of anything else I'd rather see you wearing," he replied, nibbling her lips. "It'll be so grand…."

She laughed. "Two hundred grand?"

"No. Just one."

"One *what?*"

"Canyon."

"The one in Arizona?"

"The very one."

"Noah, I've always dreamed of seeing it."

"That's what I'm here for," he promised, "to make all of your dreams come true."

"Suddenly," Dara said, smiling, "I feel *very* married."

* * * * *

Dear Reader,

Americans love to root for the underdog. Why? Maybe because right from the beginning we've been a nation determined to beat the odds.

Some of the most courageous underdogs in our history were the brave young couples who sacrificed dreams of romantic love to submit to arranged marriages.

That practice may seem heartless to us now, but only until we realize how different life was for our grandparents and great-grandparents, whose happy endings came from doing what was best for their families…and boundless belief in the Creator.…

My maternal grandparents were the products of such a union. Young, naive, unable to speak English, my grandpa, Francesco Citerony, came to the New World to make a life for himself and the shy girl who waited for him in the Old Country. When the time was right, he sent for his Theresa. Romantic love wasn't foremost in their minds during those early years of struggle and toil, but a deep and abiding love grew from the roots of their self-sacrifice. Their love endured and intensified… even outliving Grandpa, who died shortly after their thirtieth anniversary.

Their love story inspired *Suddenly Married*.

Loree Lough

Take 2 inspirational love stories FREE!

PLUS get a FREE surprise gift!

Special Limited-Time Offer

Mail to Steeple Hill Reader Service™

In U.S.	In Canada
3010 Walden Ave.	P.O. Box 609
P.O. Box 1867	Fort Erie, Ontario
Buffalo, NY 14240-1867	L2A 5X3

YES! Please send me 2 free Love Inspired® novels and my free surprise gift. Then send me 3 brand-new novels every month, which I will receive months before they appear in bookstores. Bill me at the low price of $3.74 each in the U.S. and $3.96 each in Canada, plus 25¢ delivery and applicable sales tax, if any*. That's the complete price and a saving of over 10% off the cover prices—quite a bargain! I understand that accepting the books and gift places me under no obligation ever to buy any books. I can always return a shipment and cancel at any time. Even if I never buy another book from Steeple Hill, the 2 free books and the surprise gift are mine to keep forever.

303 IEN CM6R
103 IEN CM6Q

Name	(PLEASE PRINT)	
Address	Apt. No.	
City	State/Prov.	Zip/Postal Code

Available in February 1999 from

Love Inspired ®...

WEDDING AT WILDWOOD

by *Lenora Worth*

When Isabel Landry returns to her hometown, she is forced to come to terms with the intolerance that forced her to abandon her dreams of being with the man she has always loved.

Watch for WEDDING AT WILDWOOD in February 1999 from

® *Love Inspired* ®

Available at your favorite retail outlet.

ILIWAW